PROLOGUE

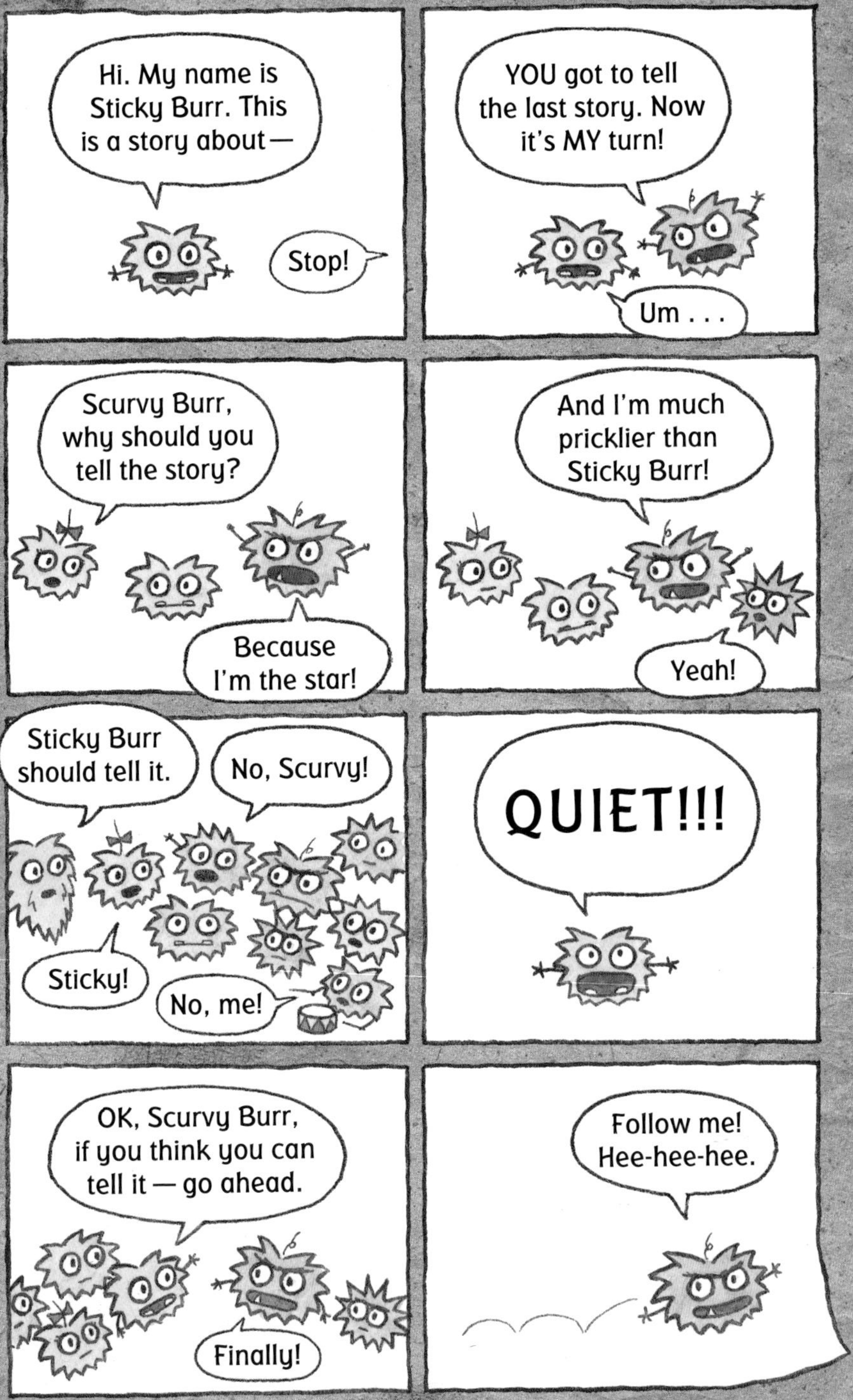
Hi. My name is Sticky Burr. This is a story about—
Stop!
YOU got to tell the last story. Now it's MY turn!
Um . . .
Scurvy Burr, why should you tell the story?
Because I'm the star!
And I'm much pricklier than Sticky Burr!
Yeah!
Sticky Burr should tell it.
No, Scurvy!
Sticky!
No, me!
QUIET!!!
OK, Scurvy Burr, if you think you can tell it — go ahead.
Finally!
Follow me! Hee-hee-hee.

For all my nieces and nephews

First paperback edition 2009

The Library of Congress has cataloged the
hardcover edition as follows:

Lechner, John, date.
Sticky Burr: the prickly peril / John Lechner. —1st ed.
p.   cm.
Summary: Scurvy and Spiny Burr team up with an exiled
and bitter burr in an attempt to take over Burrwood Village
and get rid of nice guy, Sticky Burr, once and for all.
ISBN 978-0-7636-4145-0 (hardcover)
[1. Conflict (Psychology)—Fiction. 2. Individuality—Fiction.
3. Insects—Fiction. 4. Forests and forestry—Fiction.] I. Title.
PZ7.L4846Stp 2009
[E]—dc22   2008028759

ISBN 978-0-7636-4580-9 (paperback)

09 10 11 12 13 14 SCP 10 9 8 7 6 5 4 3 2

Printed in Humen, Dongguan, China

This book was typeset in Badger and Blockhead.
The illustrations were done in watercolor and ink.

Candlewick Press
99 Dover Street
Somerville, Massachusetts 02144

visit us at www.candlewick.com

STICKY
BURR
THE PRICKLY PERIL

BURR: (n) the rough, prickly seedcase of certain plants

STICKY: (adj) tending to cling to things; difficult to deal with

MEET THE CHARACTERS

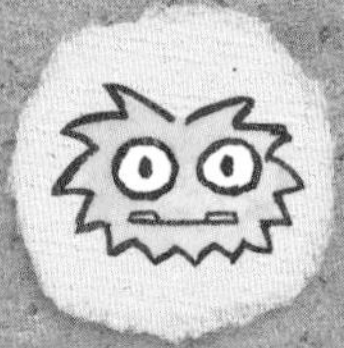
Sticky Burr

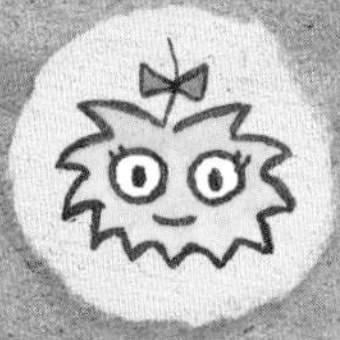
Mossy Burr

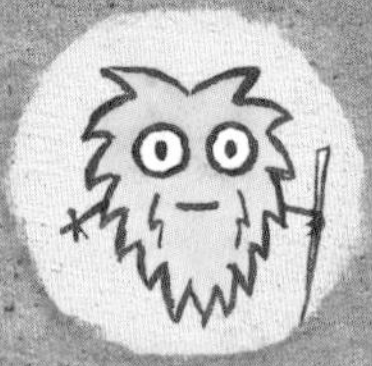
Elder Burr

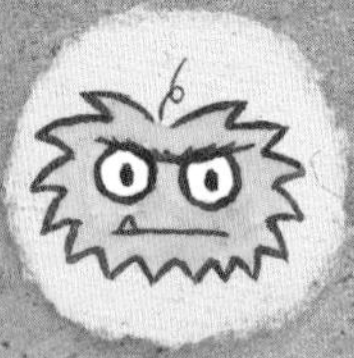
Scurvy Burr

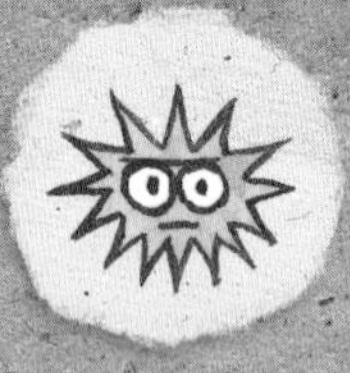
Spiny Burr

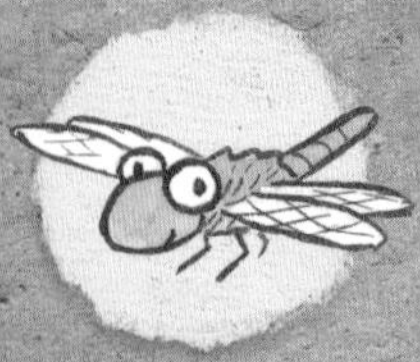
Draffle

STICKY BURR

THE PRICKLY PERIL

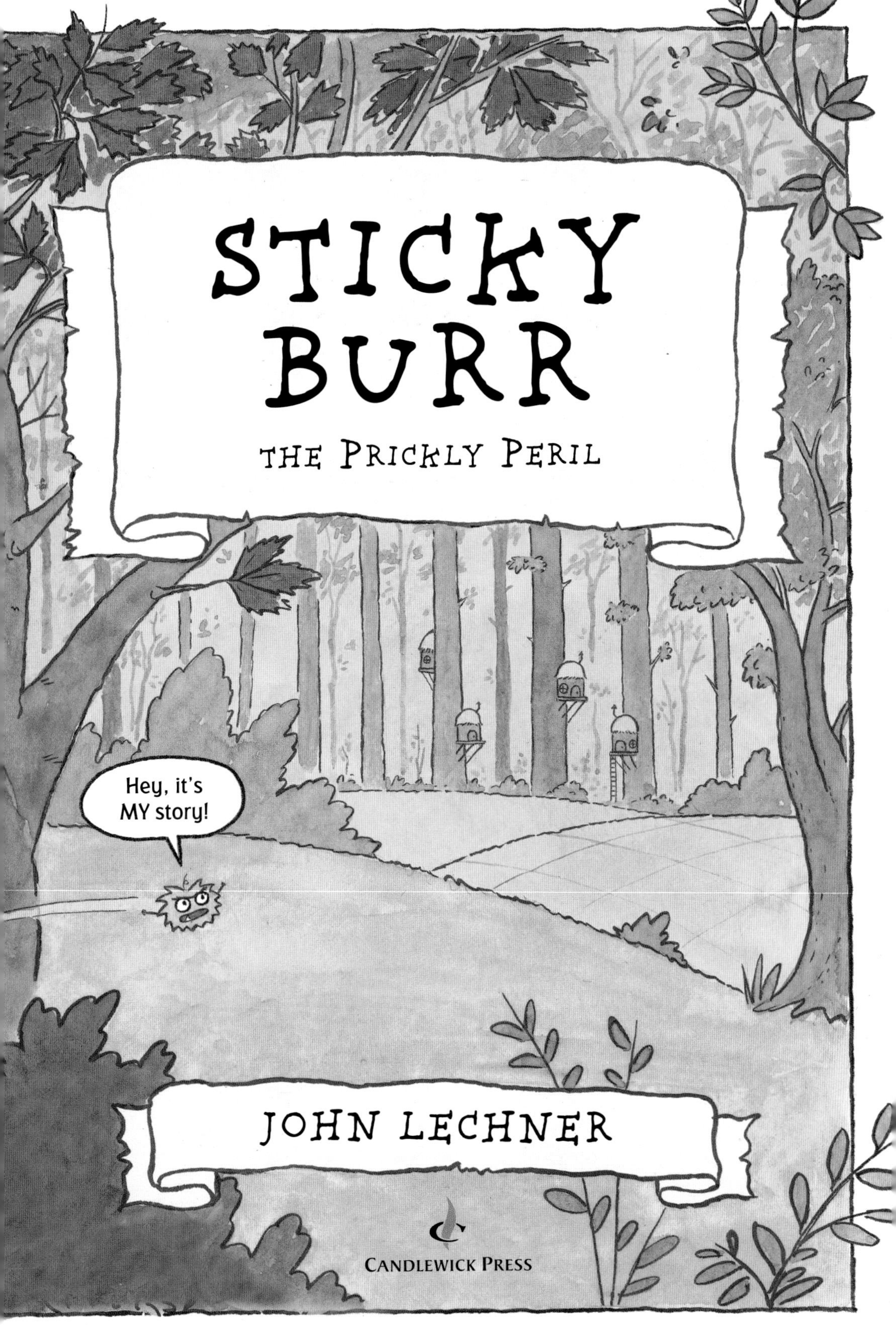
Hey, it's MY story!

JOHN LECHNER

CANDLEWICK PRESS

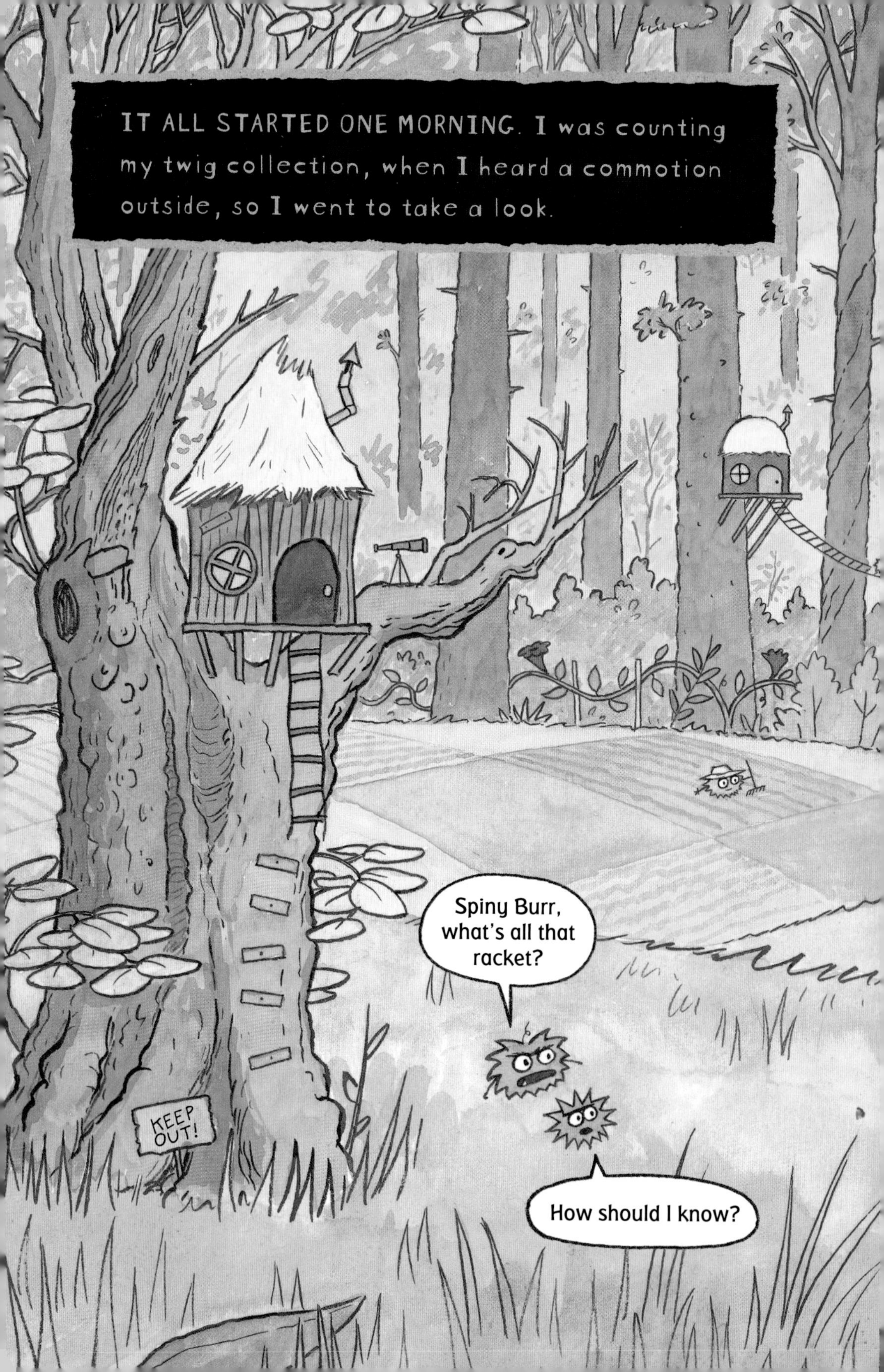
IT ALL STARTED ONE MORNING. I was counting my twig collection, when I heard a commotion outside, so I went to take a look.
Spiny Burr, what's all that racket?
How should I know?
KEEP OUT!

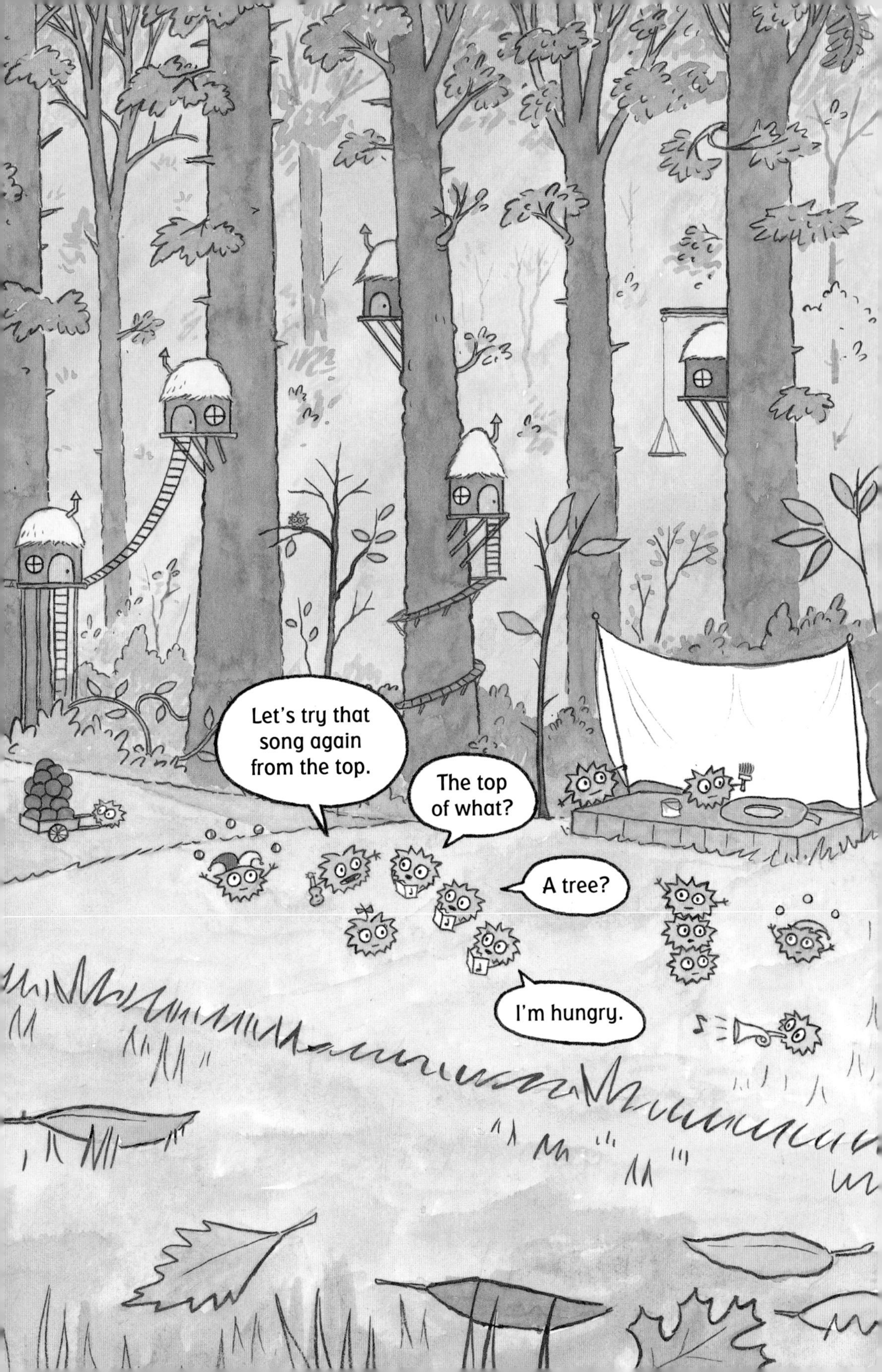
Let's try that song again from the top.
The top of what?
A tree?
I'm hungry.

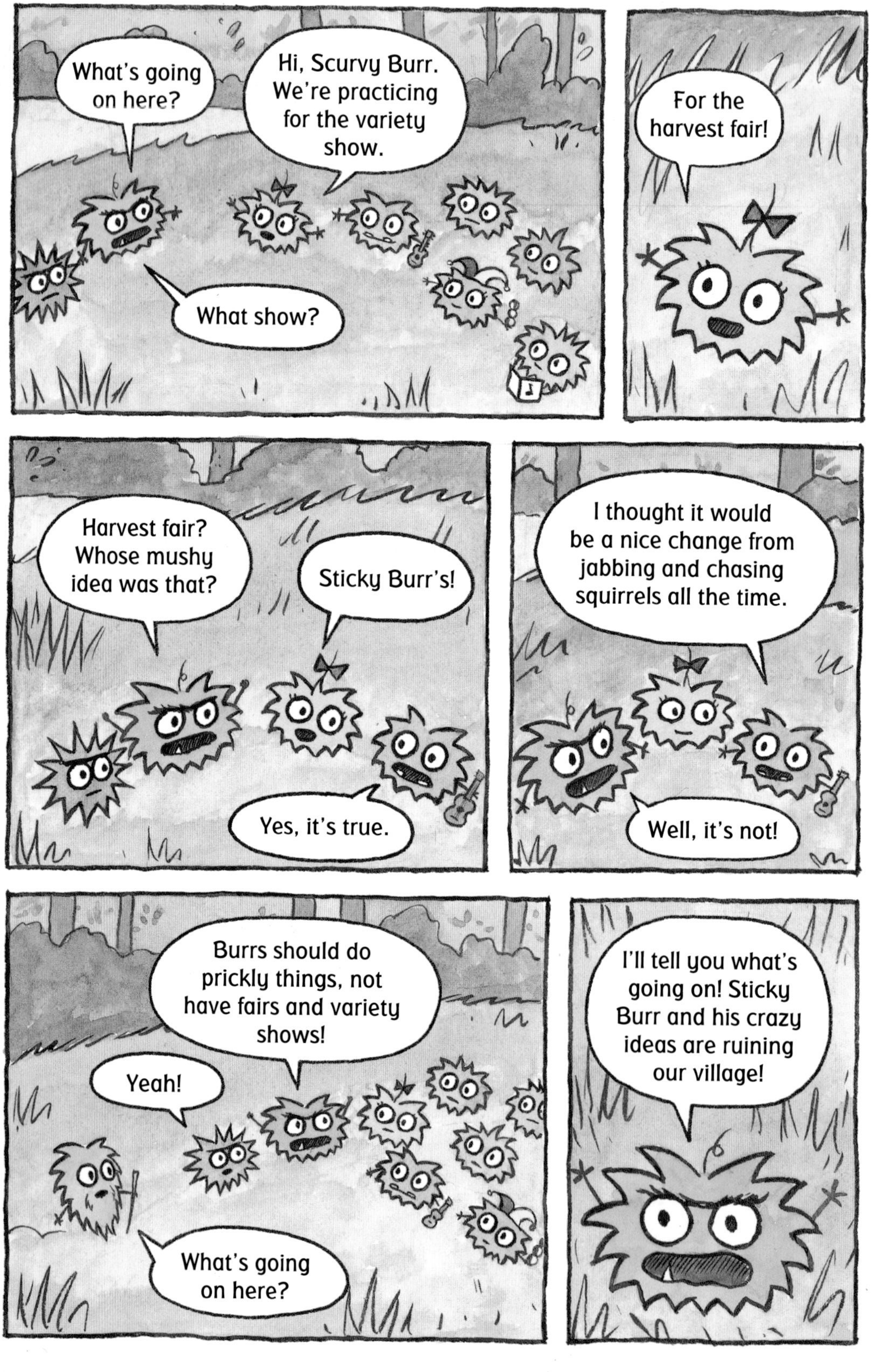
What's going on here?
Hi, Scurvy Burr. We're practicing for the variety show.
What show?
For the harvest fair!
Harvest fair? Whose mushy idea was that?
Sticky Burr's!
Yes, it's true.
I thought it would be a nice change from jabbing and chasing squirrels all the time.
Well, it's not!
Burrs should do prickly things, not have fairs and variety shows!
Yeah!
What's going on here?
I'll tell you what's going on! Sticky Burr and his crazy ideas are ruining our village!

SCURVY BURR'S JOURNAL

OK, this is MY story, and I'm going to tell you about burrs. We are prickly and covered with tiny hooks, so we stick to things.

Me in a bad mood

We like to do prickly things, like jab squirrels,

chase small animals,

and just be prickly through and through.

This is NOT how Sticky Burr behaves! All he does is paint pictures and play the ukulele and spread his cheerful nonsense. It drives me crazy!

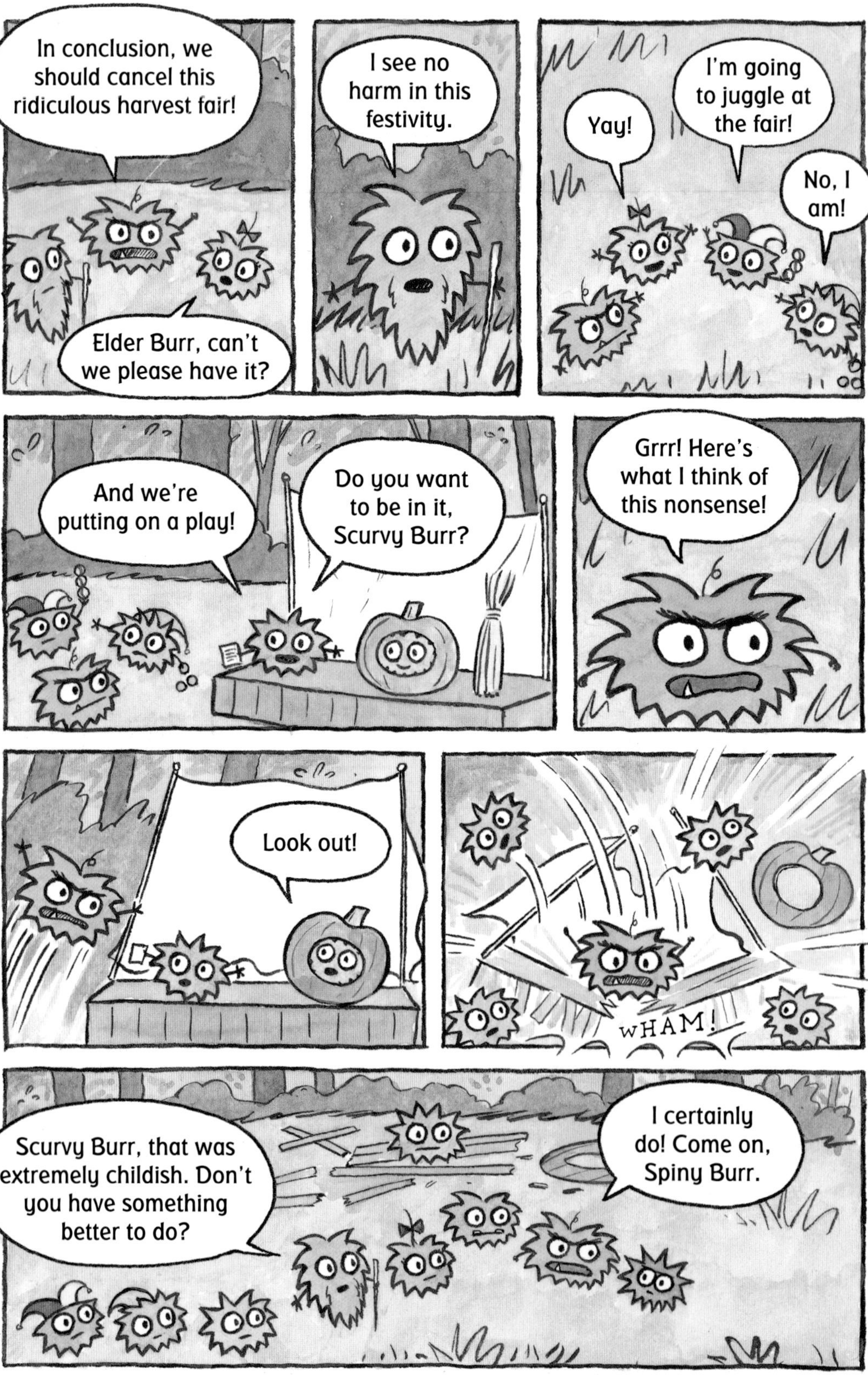
In conclusion, we should cancel this ridiculous harvest fair!
Elder Burr, can't we please have it?
I see no harm in this festivity.
Yay!
I'm going to juggle at the fair!
No, I am!
And we're putting on a play!
Do you want to be in it, Scurvy Burr?
Grrr! Here's what I think of this nonsense!
Look out!
WHAM!
Scurvy Burr, that was extremely childish. Don't you have something better to do?
I certainly do! Come on, Spiny Burr.

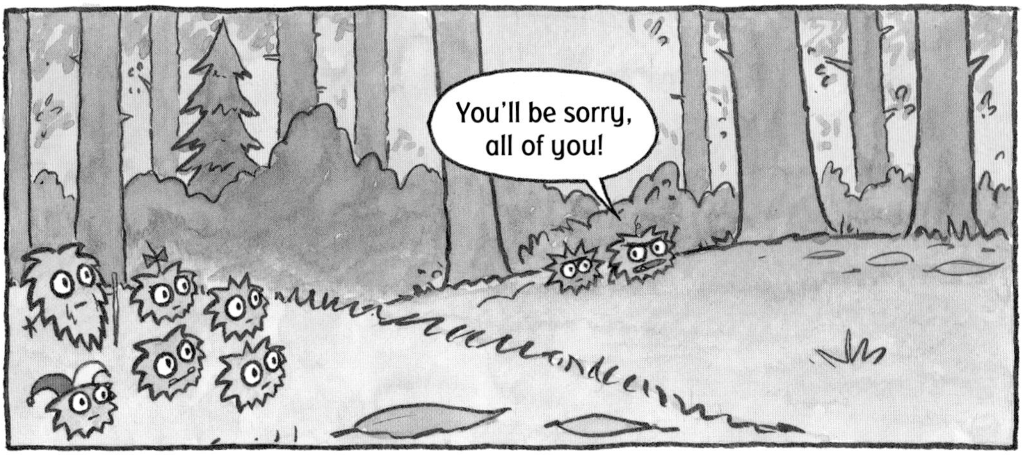
You'll be sorry, all of you!

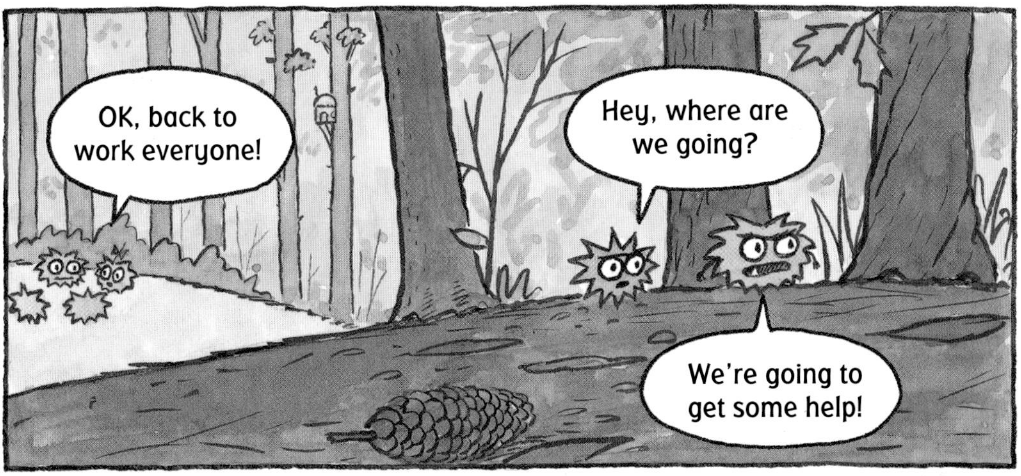
OK, back to work everyone!
Hey, where are we going?
We're going to get some help!

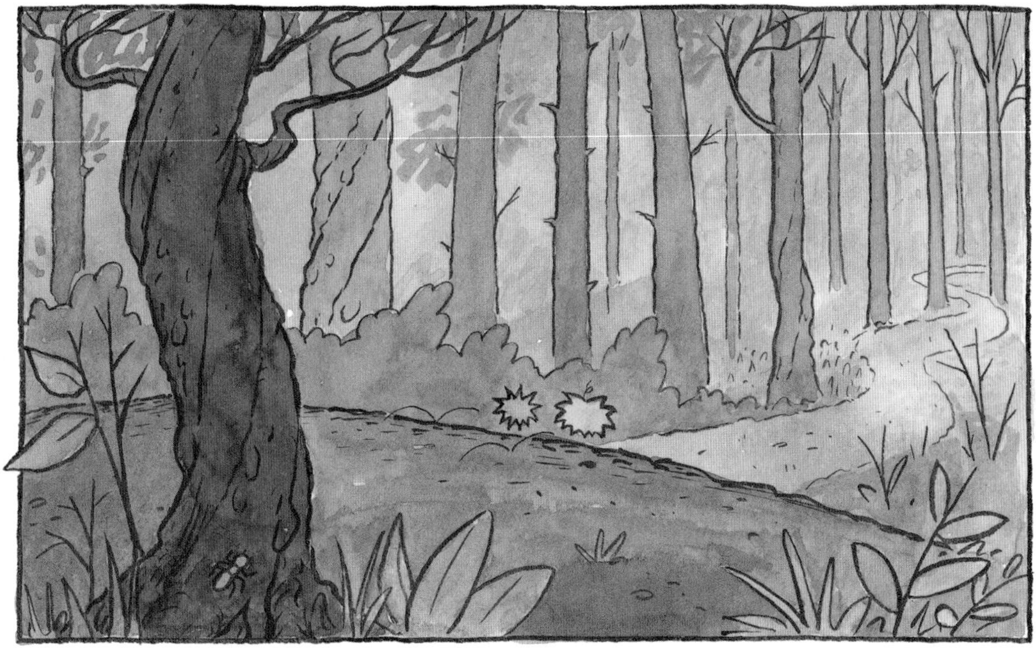

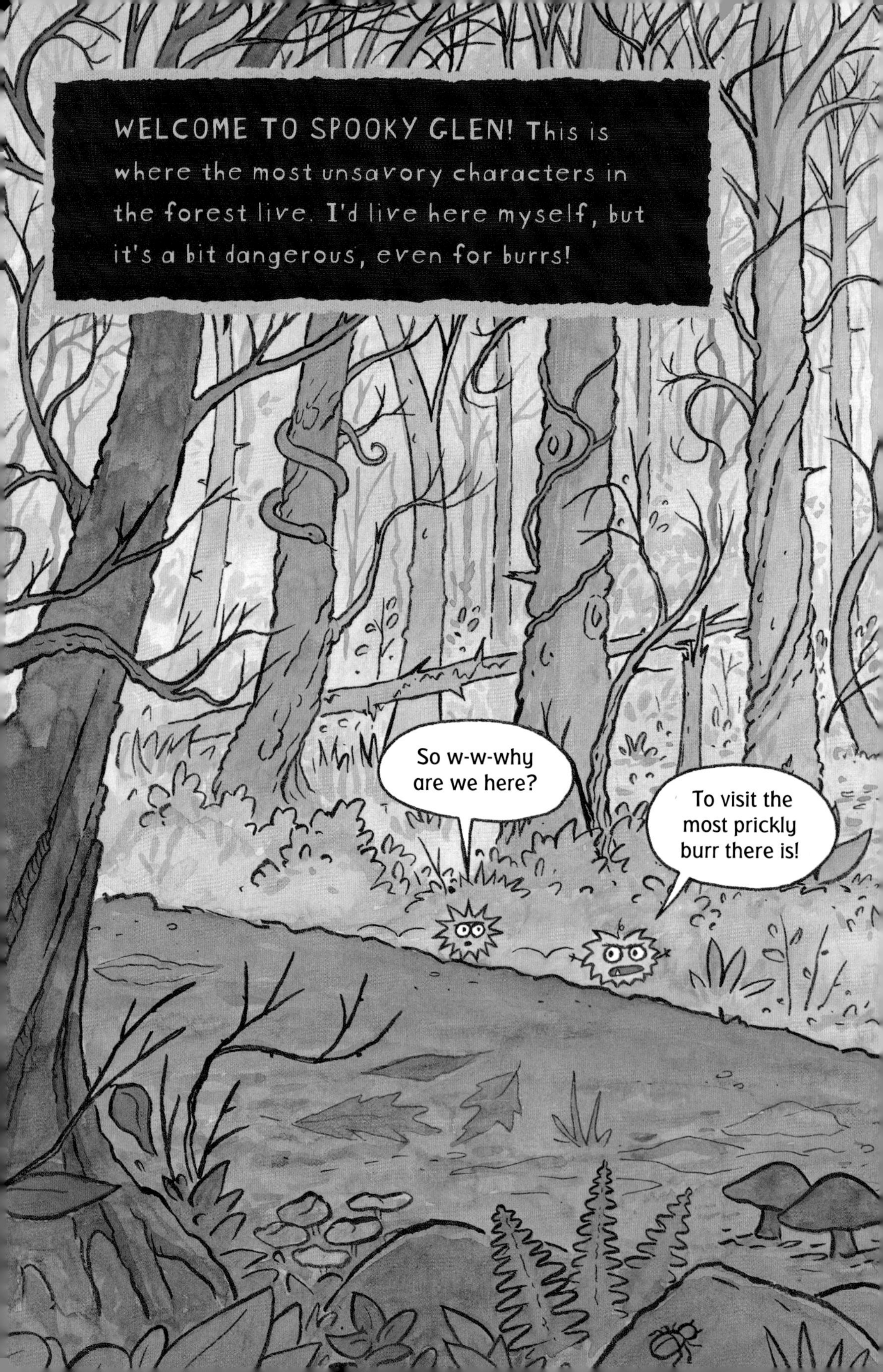
WELCOME TO SPOOKY GLEN! This is where the most unsavory characters in the forest live. I'd live here myself, but it's a bit dangerous, even for burrs!
So w-w-why are we here?
To visit the most prickly burr there is!

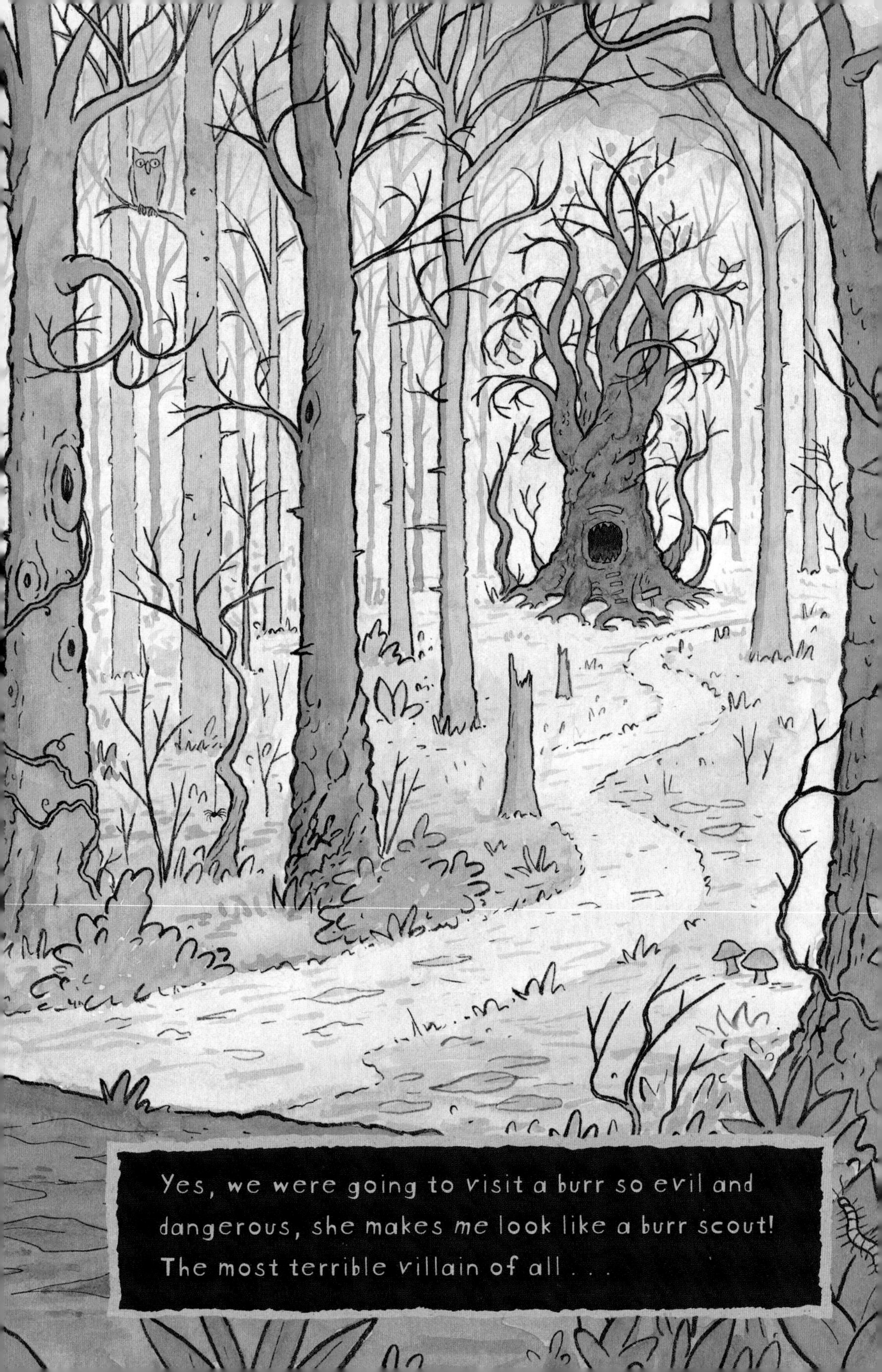
Yes, we were going to visit a burr so evil and dangerous, she makes *me* look like a burr scout! The most terrible villain of all . . .

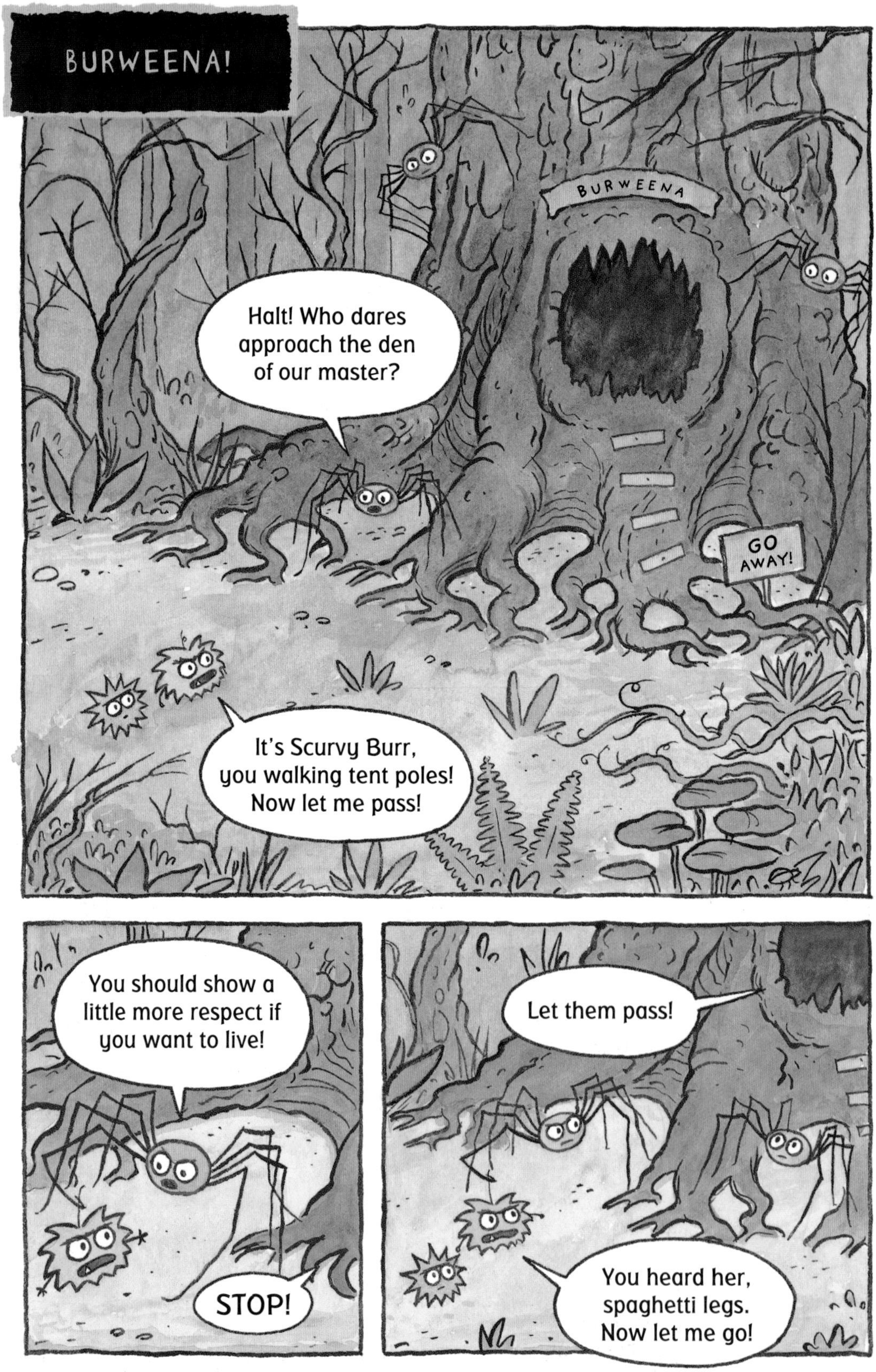
BURWEENA!
BURWEENA
Halt! Who dares approach the den of our master?
GO AWAY!
It's Scurvy Burr, you walking tent poles! Now let me pass!
You should show a little more respect if you want to live!
STOP!
Let them pass!
You heard her, spaghetti legs. Now let me go!

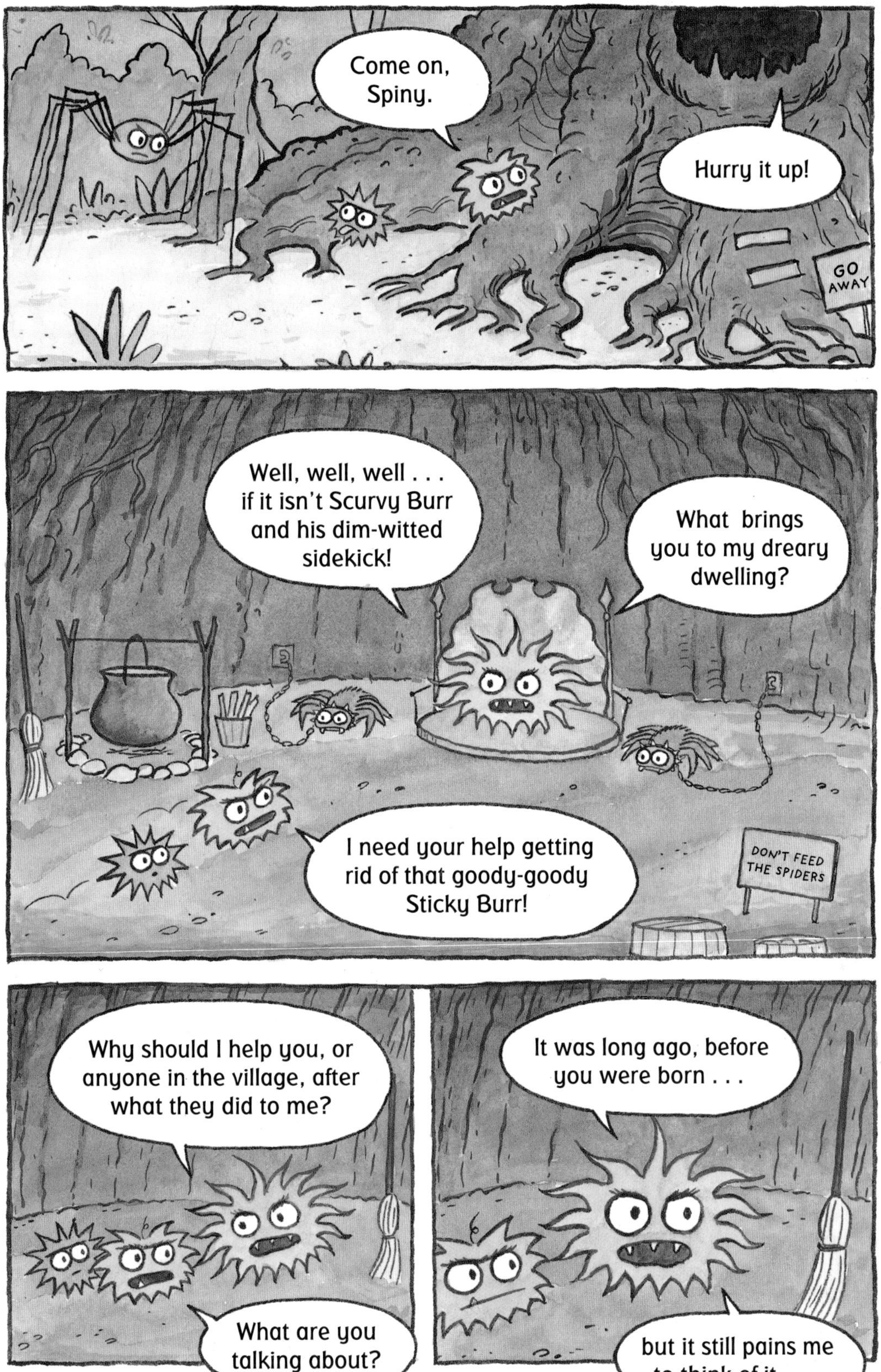

Come on, Spiny.
Hurry it up!
GO AWAY
Well, well, well . . . if it isn't Scurvy Burr and his dim-witted sidekick!
What brings you to my dreary dwelling?
I need your help getting rid of that goody-goody Sticky Burr!
DON'T FEED THE SPIDERS
Why should I help you, or anyone in the village, after what they did to me?
What are you talking about?
It was long ago, before you were born . . .
but it still pains me to think of it. . . .

THE STORY OF BURWEENA
AS TOLD TO SCURVY BURR

I was born like most burrs, by falling out of a tree. But unlike most baby burrs, no one wanted me.

I was just too prickly!

Waaah!

Um . . . you take her!

And I also liked to play pranks.

Wah!

TRIP!

I was a thorn in everyone's side.

Wa-ha-ha!

I grew up to be even more prickly.

Grrr!

!

The leader of the village at the time, Sickly Burr, was very ill, and a new leader had not been chosen yet.

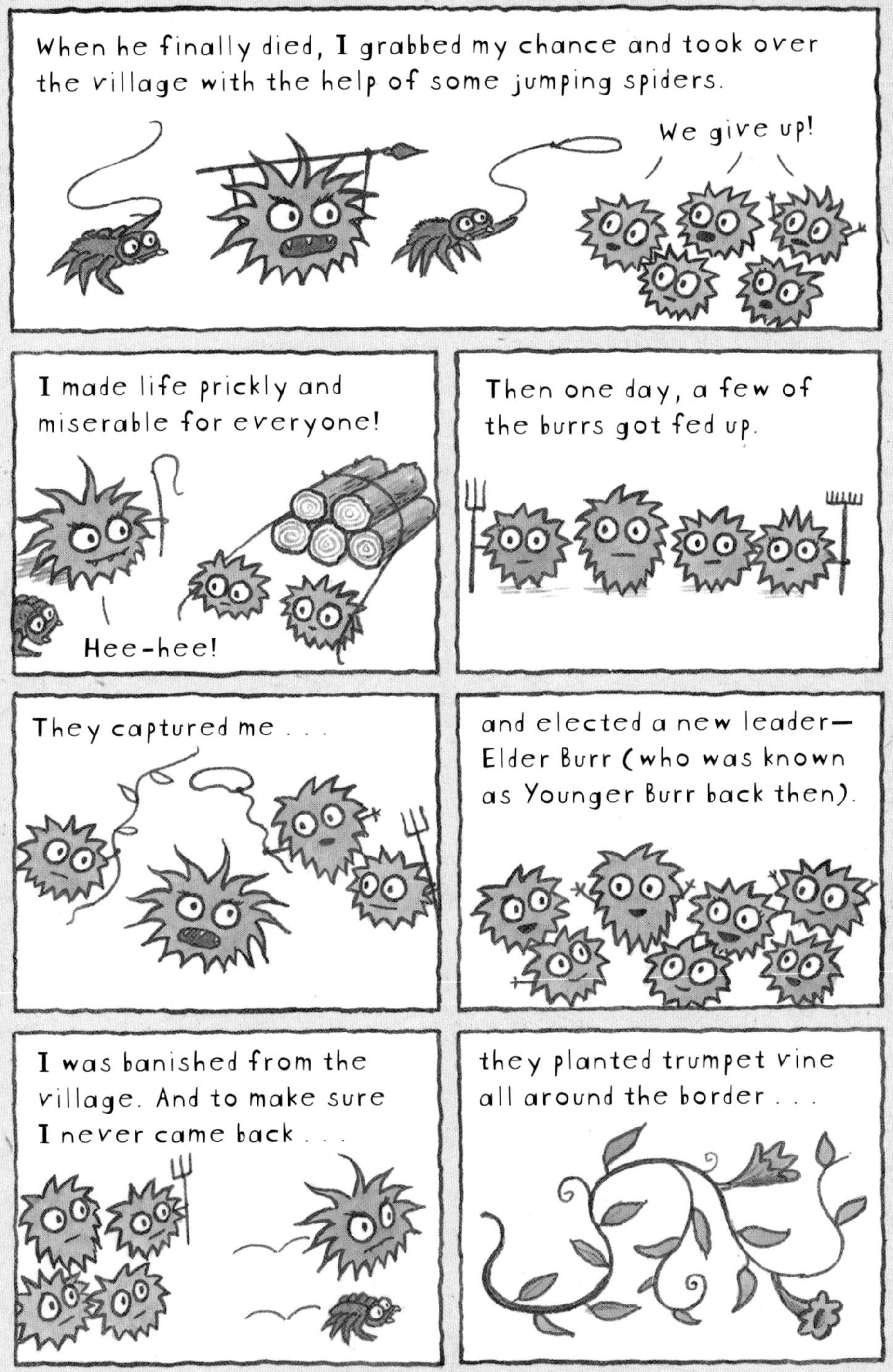
When he finally died, I grabbed my chance and took over the village with the help of some jumping spiders.
We give up!
I made life prickly and miserable for everyone!
Hee-hee!
Then one day, a few of the burrs got fed up.
They captured me . . .
and elected a new leader— Elder Burr (who was known as Younger Burr back then).
I was banished from the village. And to make sure I never came back . . .
they planted trumpet vine all around the border . . .

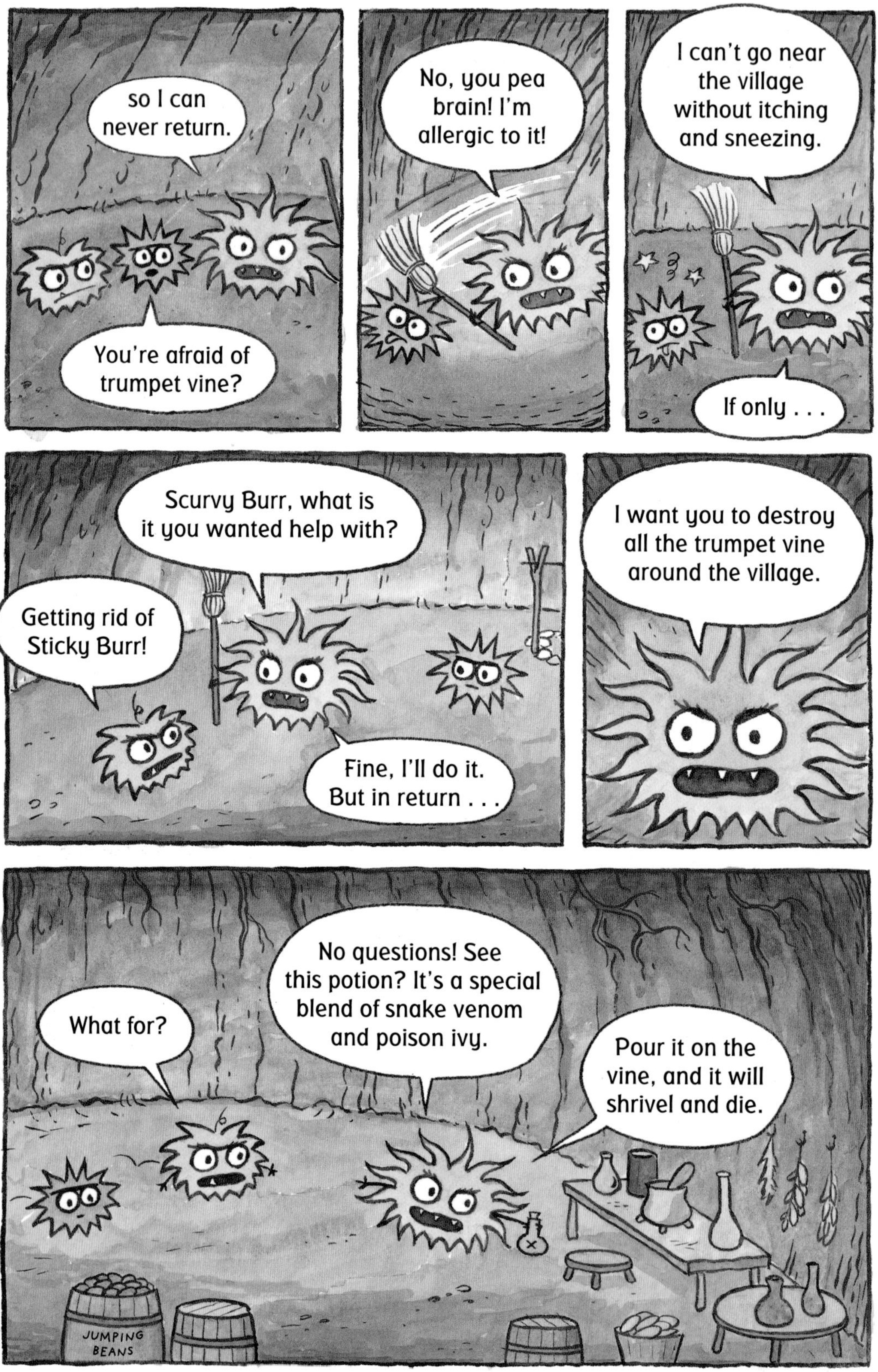
so I can never return.
You're afraid of trumpet vine?
No, you pea brain! I'm allergic to it!
I can't go near the village without itching and sneezing.
If only . . .
Scurvy Burr, what is it you wanted help with?
Getting rid of Sticky Burr!
Fine, I'll do it. But in return . . .
I want you to destroy all the trumpet vine around the village.
What for?
No questions! See this potion? It's a special blend of snake venom and poison ivy.
Pour it on the vine, and it will shrivel and die.
JUMPING BEANS

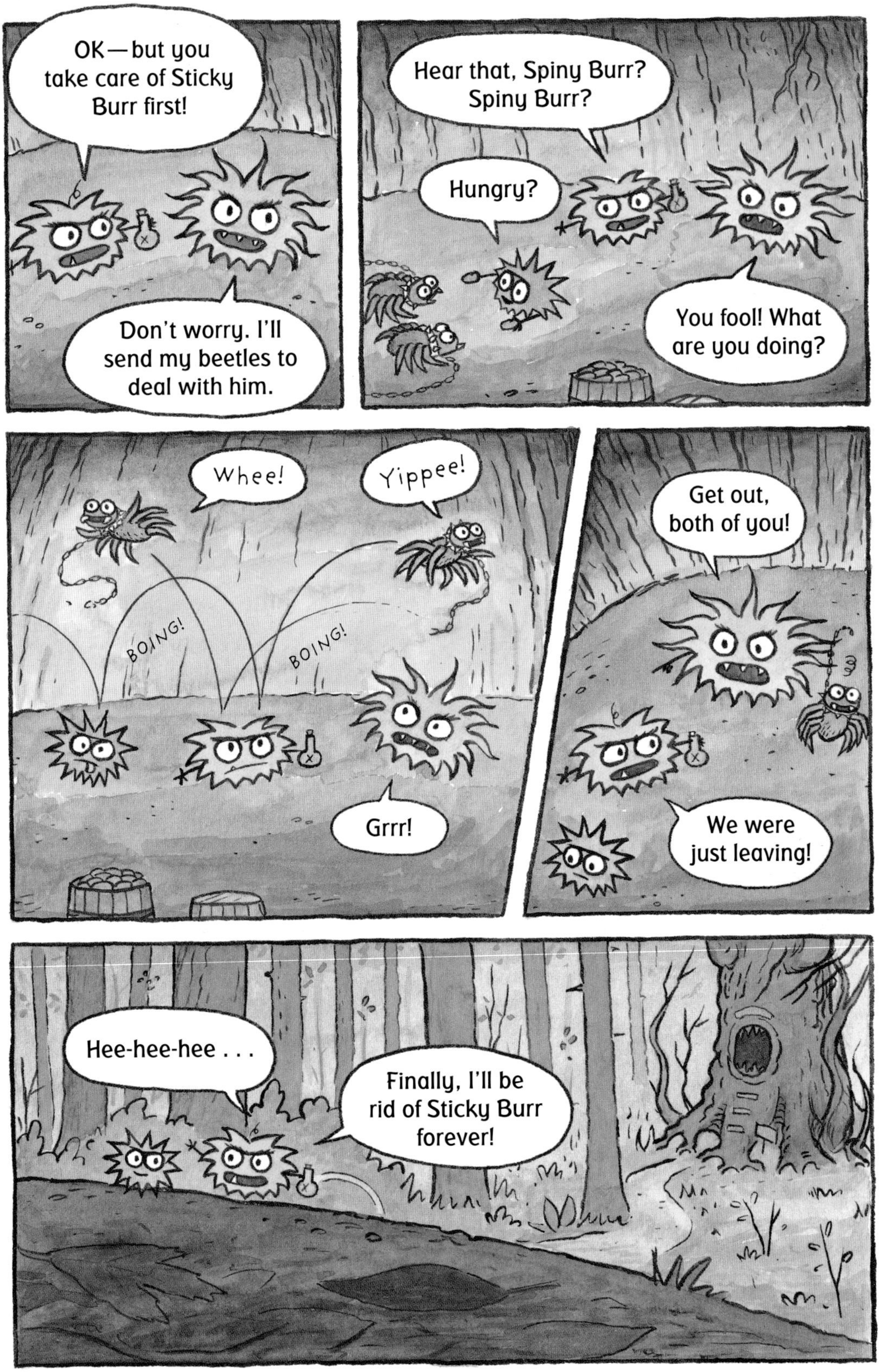

OK—but you take care of Sticky Burr first!
Don't worry. I'll send my beetles to deal with him.
Hear that, Spiny Burr? Spiny Burr?
Hungry?
You fool! What are you doing?
Whee!
Yippee!
BOING!
BOING!
Grrr!
Get out, both of you!
We were just leaving!
Hee-hee-hee . . .
Finally, I'll be rid of Sticky Burr forever!

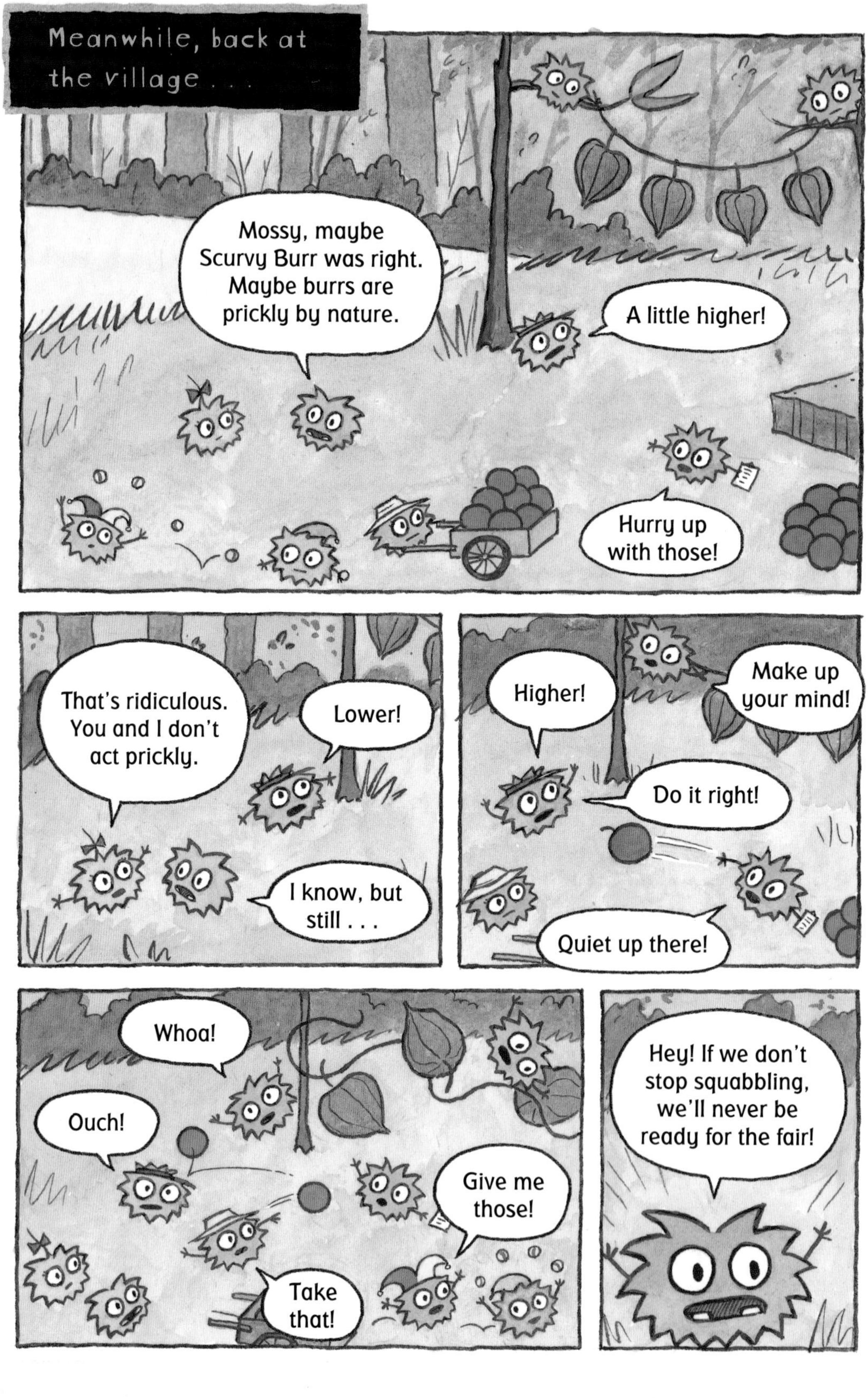
Meanwhile, back at the village . . .
Mossy, maybe Scurvy Burr was right. Maybe burrs are prickly by nature.
A little higher!
Hurry up with those!
That's ridiculous. You and I don't act prickly.
Lower!
I know, but still . . .
Higher!
Make up your mind!
Do it right!
Quiet up there!
Whoa!
Ouch!
Give me those!
Take that!
Hey! If we don't stop squabbling, we'll never be ready for the fair!

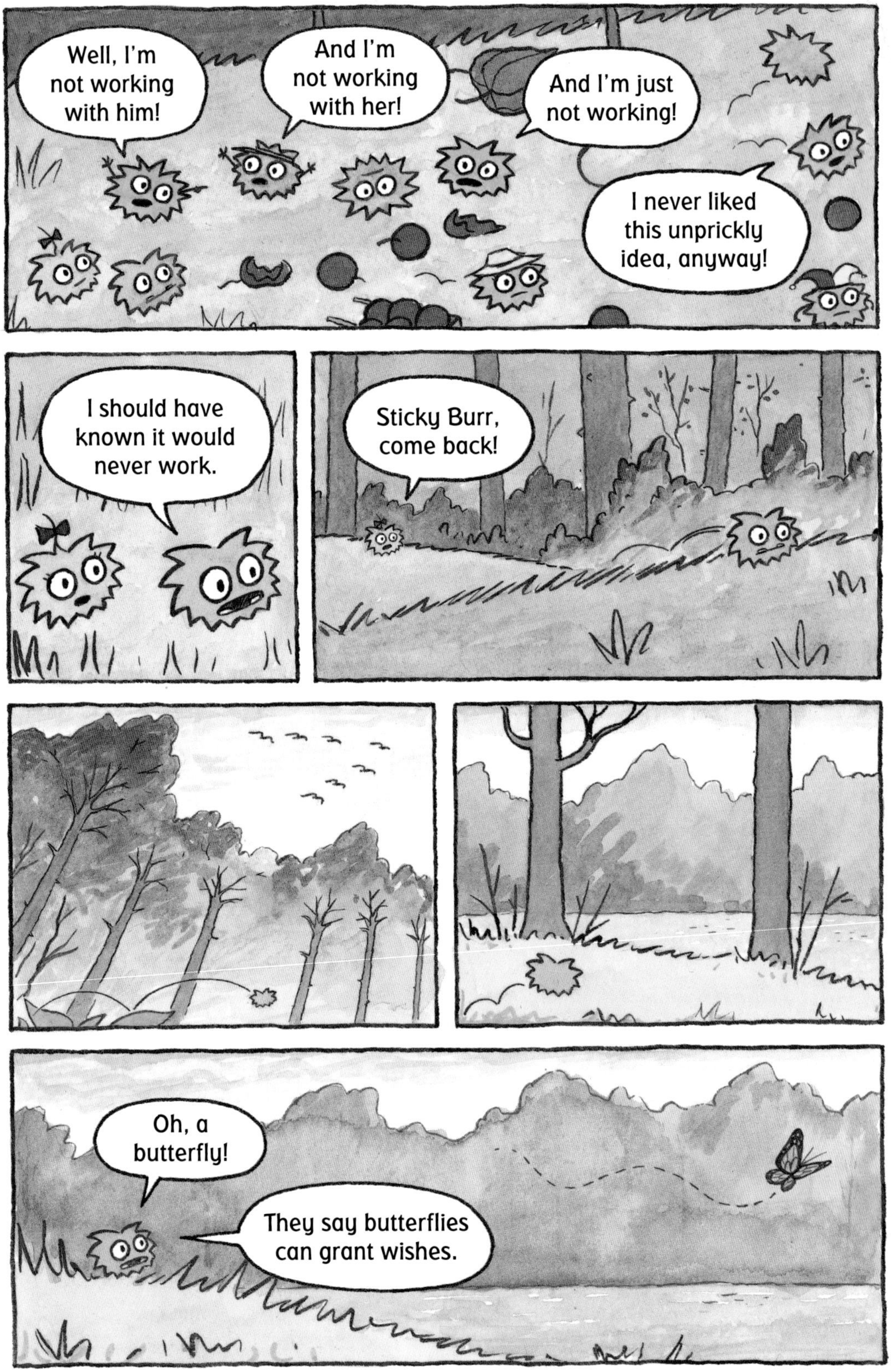
Well, I'm not working with him!
And I'm not working with her!
And I'm just not working!
I never liked this unprickly idea, anyway!
I should have known it would never work.
Sticky Burr, come back!
Oh, a butterfly!
They say butterflies can grant wishes.

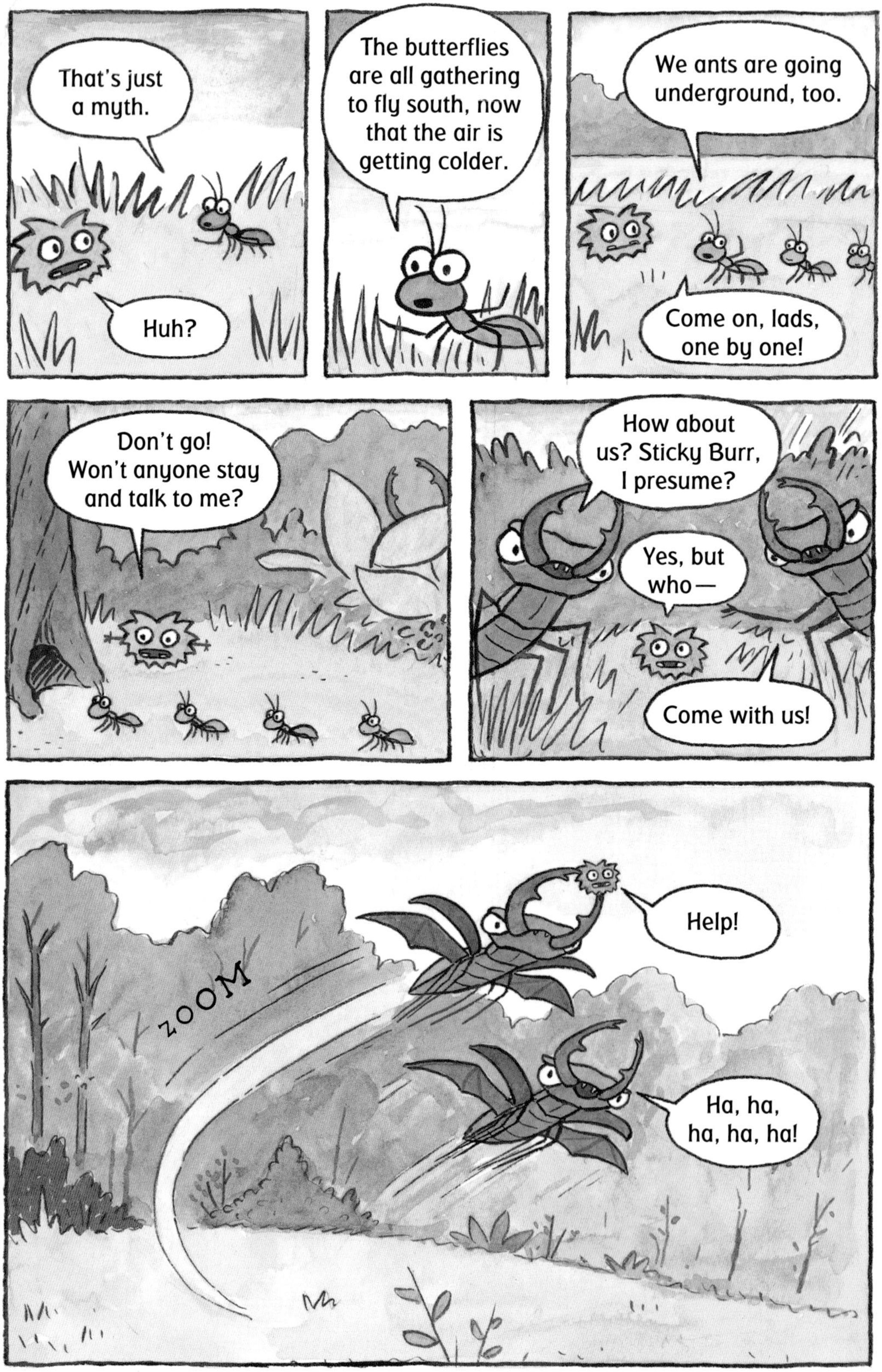

That's just a myth.
Huh?
The butterflies are all gathering to fly south, now that the air is getting colder.
We ants are going underground, too.
Come on, lads, one by one!
Don't go! Won't anyone stay and talk to me?
How about us? Sticky Burr, I presume?
Yes, but who —
Come with us!
ZOOM
Help!
Ha, ha, ha, ha, ha!

MEET THE BEETLES

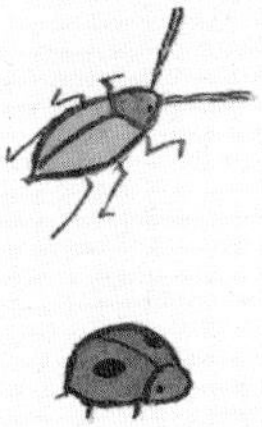

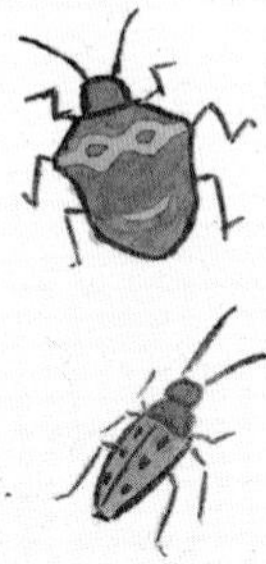

I detest beetles. Did you know that there are over 350,000 different kinds in the world? I've only met about seven.

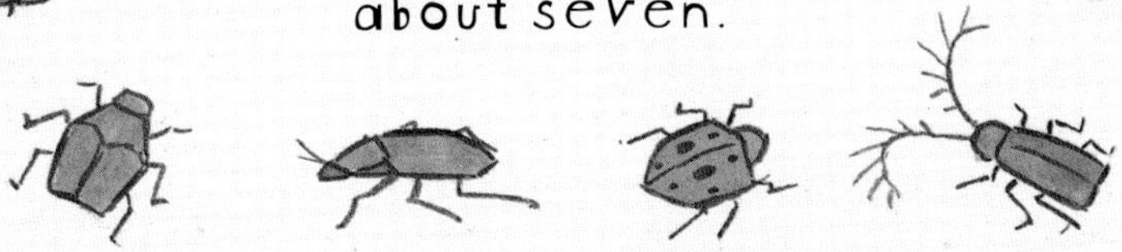

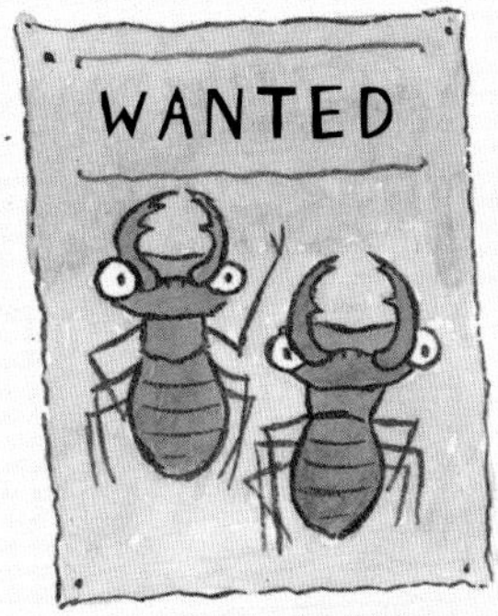
WANTED

Most stag beetles are empty-headed fools who drink fruit juice all day. But Benjamin and Barnaby are dangerous henchmen of Burweena and always up to no good.

Spooky Glen has lots of spiders, too. They try to look tough, but mostly they are blustering cowards, running away from anything bigger than they are.

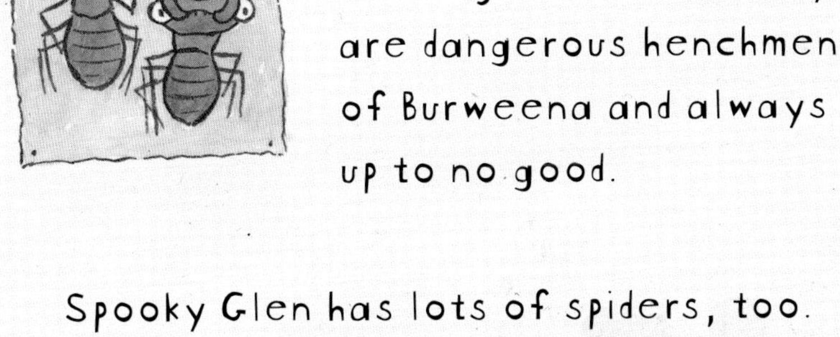
FEED ME

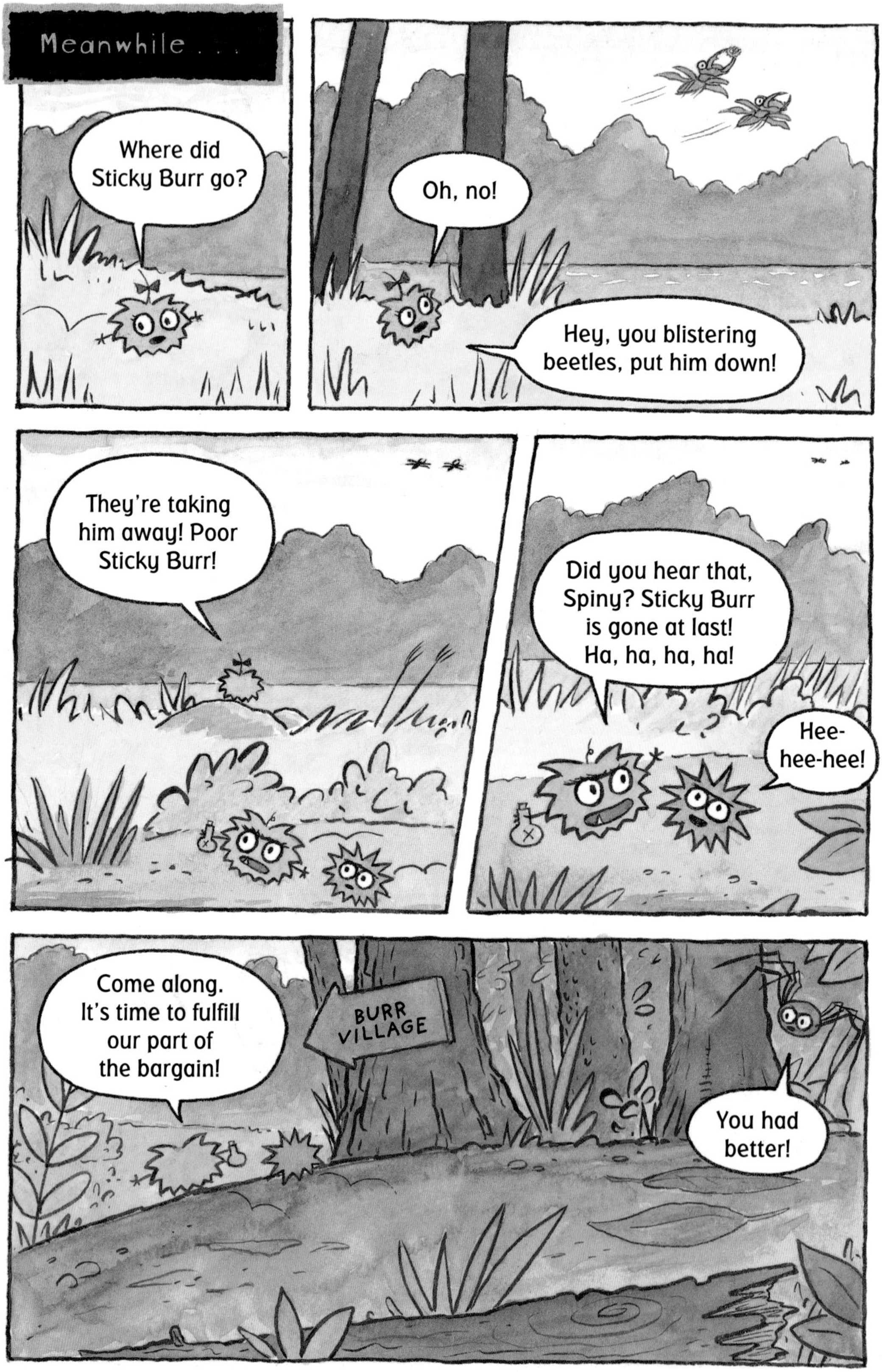
Meanwhile . . .
Where did Sticky Burr go?
Oh, no!
Hey, you blistering beetles, put him down!
They're taking him away! Poor Sticky Burr!
Did you hear that, Spiny? Sticky Burr is gone at last! Ha, ha, ha, ha!
Hee-hee-hee!
Come along. It's time to fulfill our part of the bargain!
BURR VILLAGE
You had better!

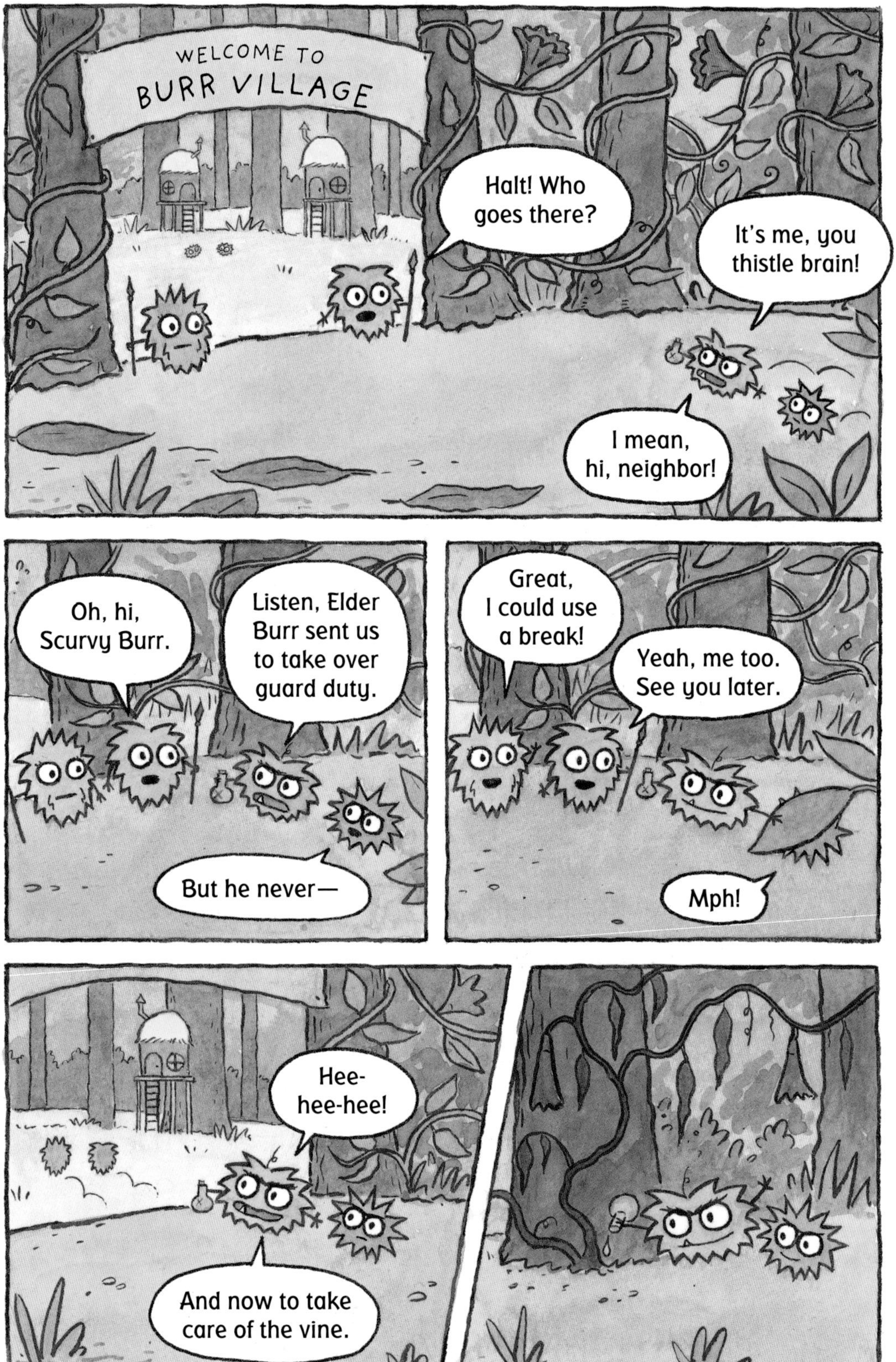
WELCOME TO
BURR VILLAGE
Halt! Who goes there?
It's me, you thistle brain!
I mean, hi, neighbor!
Oh, hi, Scurvy Burr.
Listen, Elder Burr sent us to take over guard duty.
But he never—
Great, I could use a break!
Yeah, me too. See you later.
Mph!
Hee-hee-hee!
And now to take care of the vine.

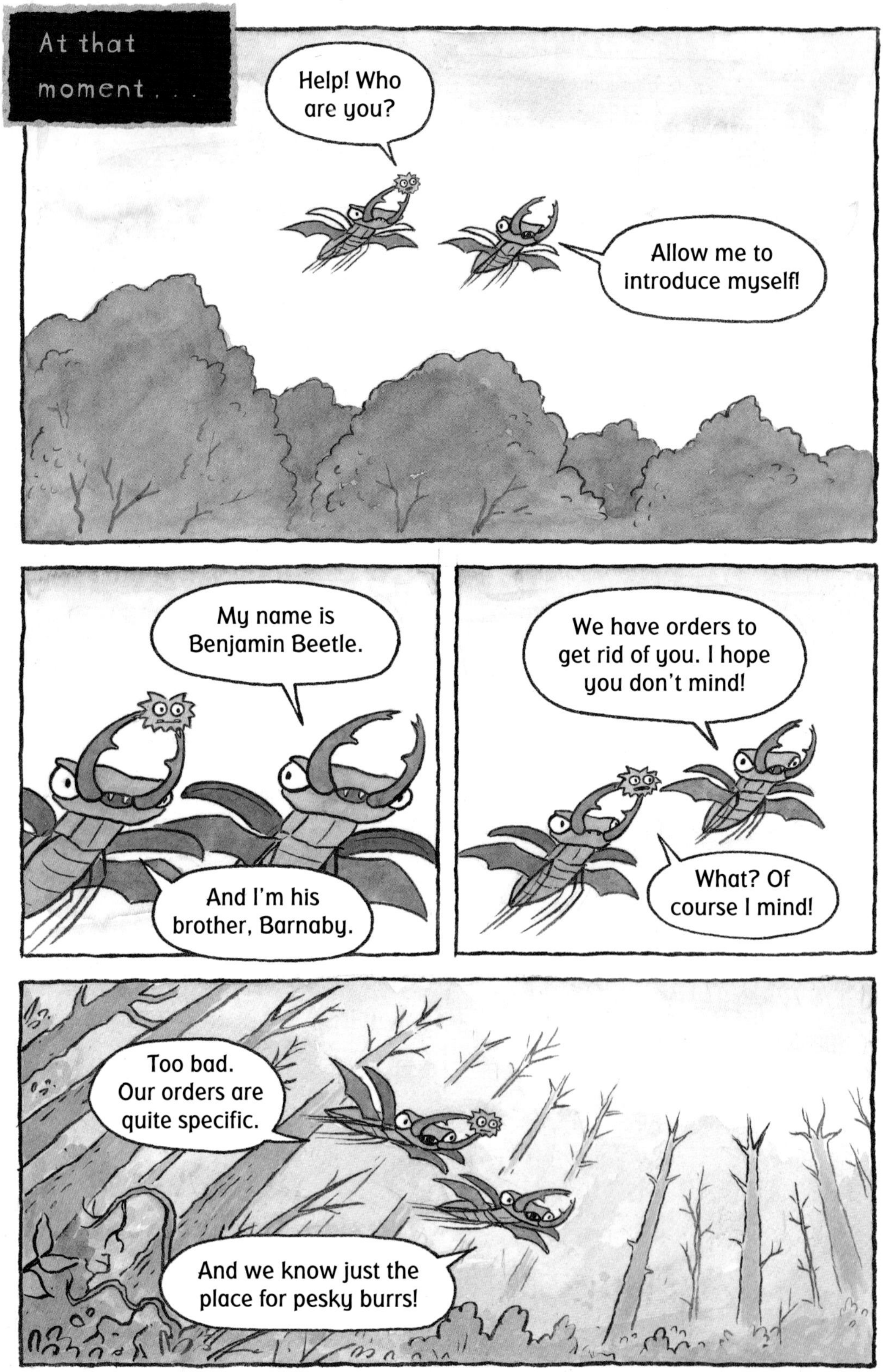
At that moment . . .
Help! Who are you?
Allow me to introduce myself!
My name is Benjamin Beetle.
And I'm his brother, Barnaby.
We have orders to get rid of you. I hope you don't mind!
What? Of course I mind!
Too bad. Our orders are quite specific.
And we know just the place for pesky burrs!

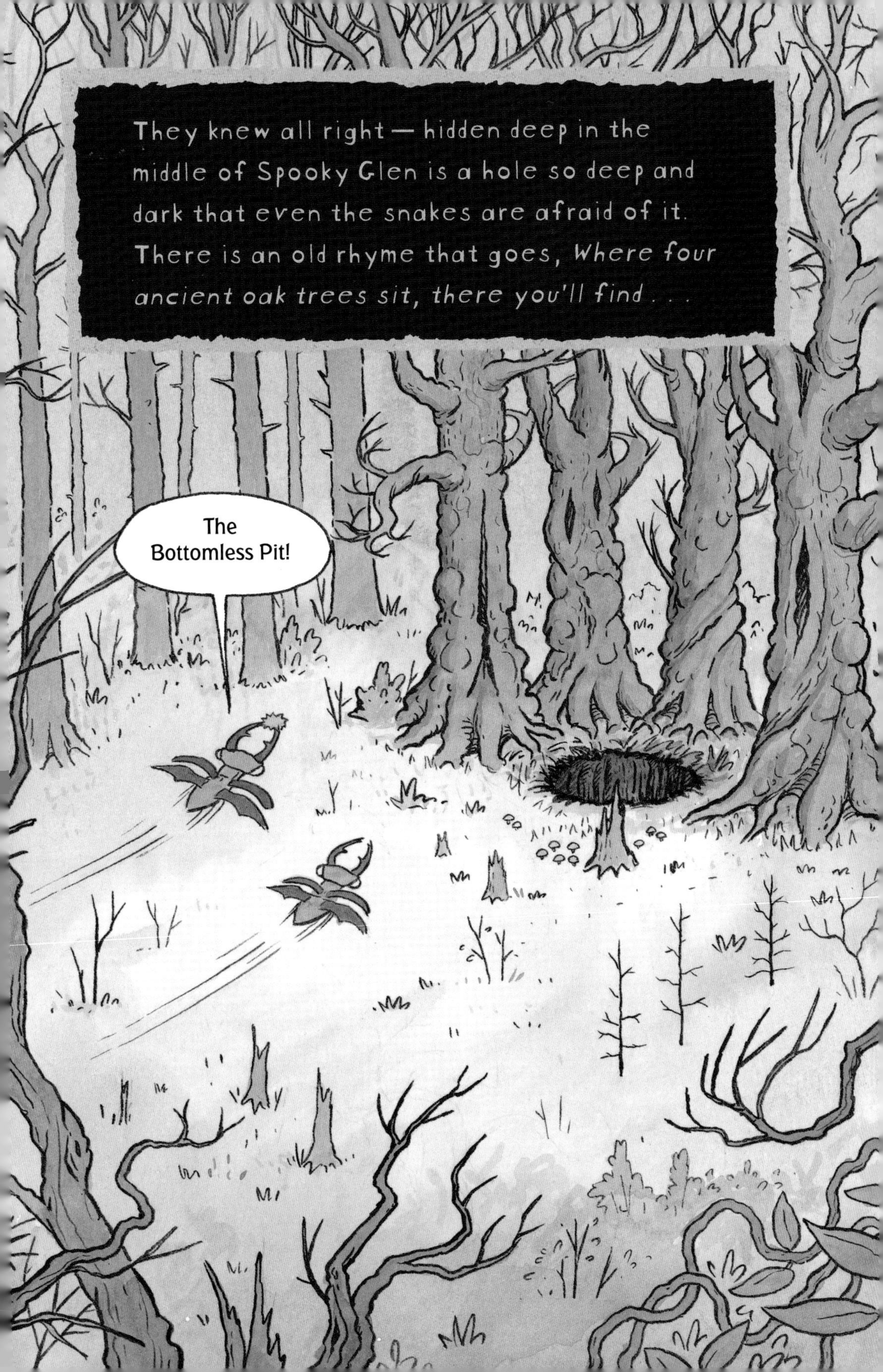
They knew all right — hidden deep in the middle of Spooky Glen is a hole so deep and dark that even the snakes are afraid of it. There is an old rhyme that goes, *Where four ancient oak trees sit, there you'll find . . .*
The Bottomless Pit!

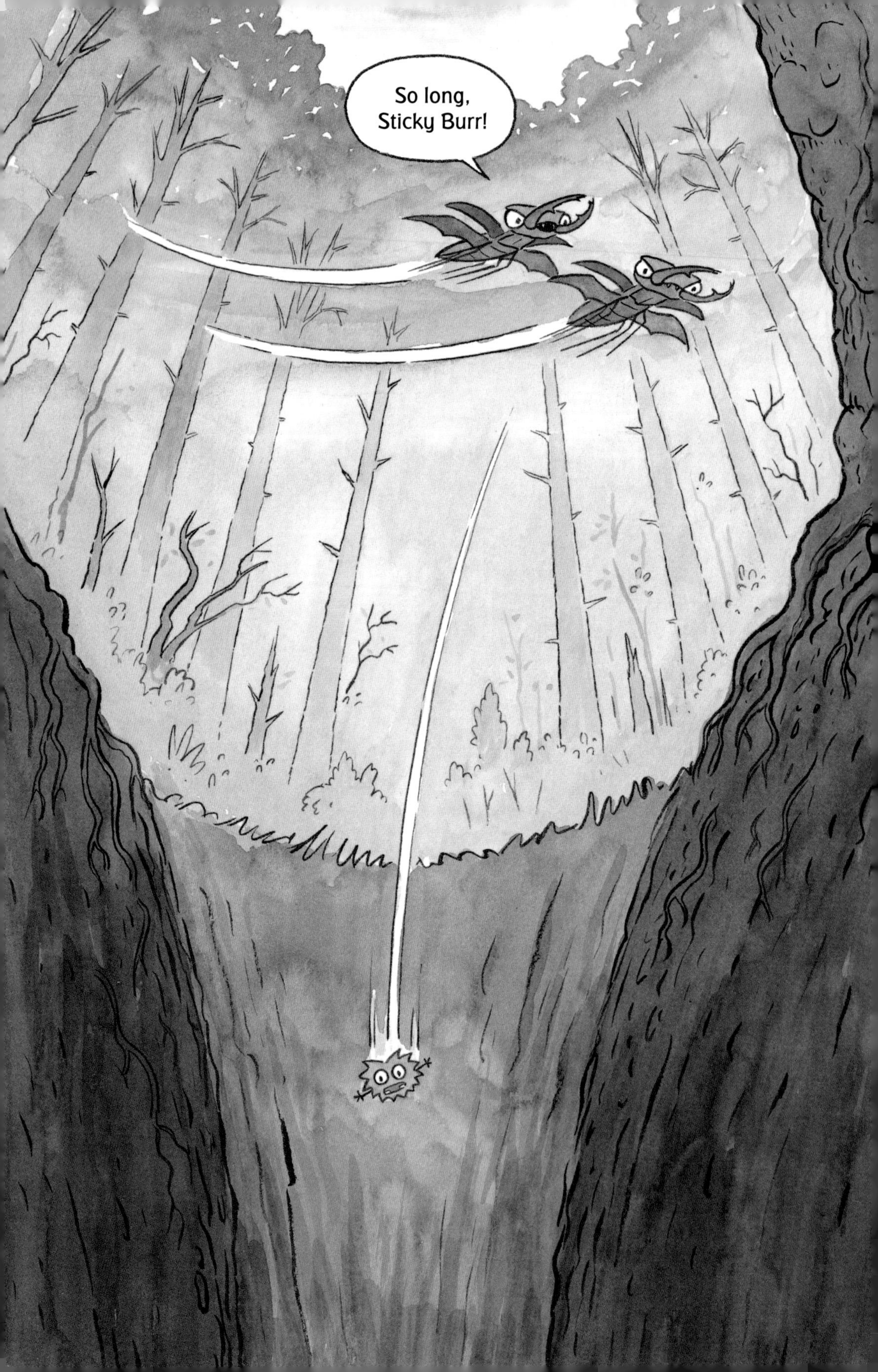
So long, Sticky Burr!

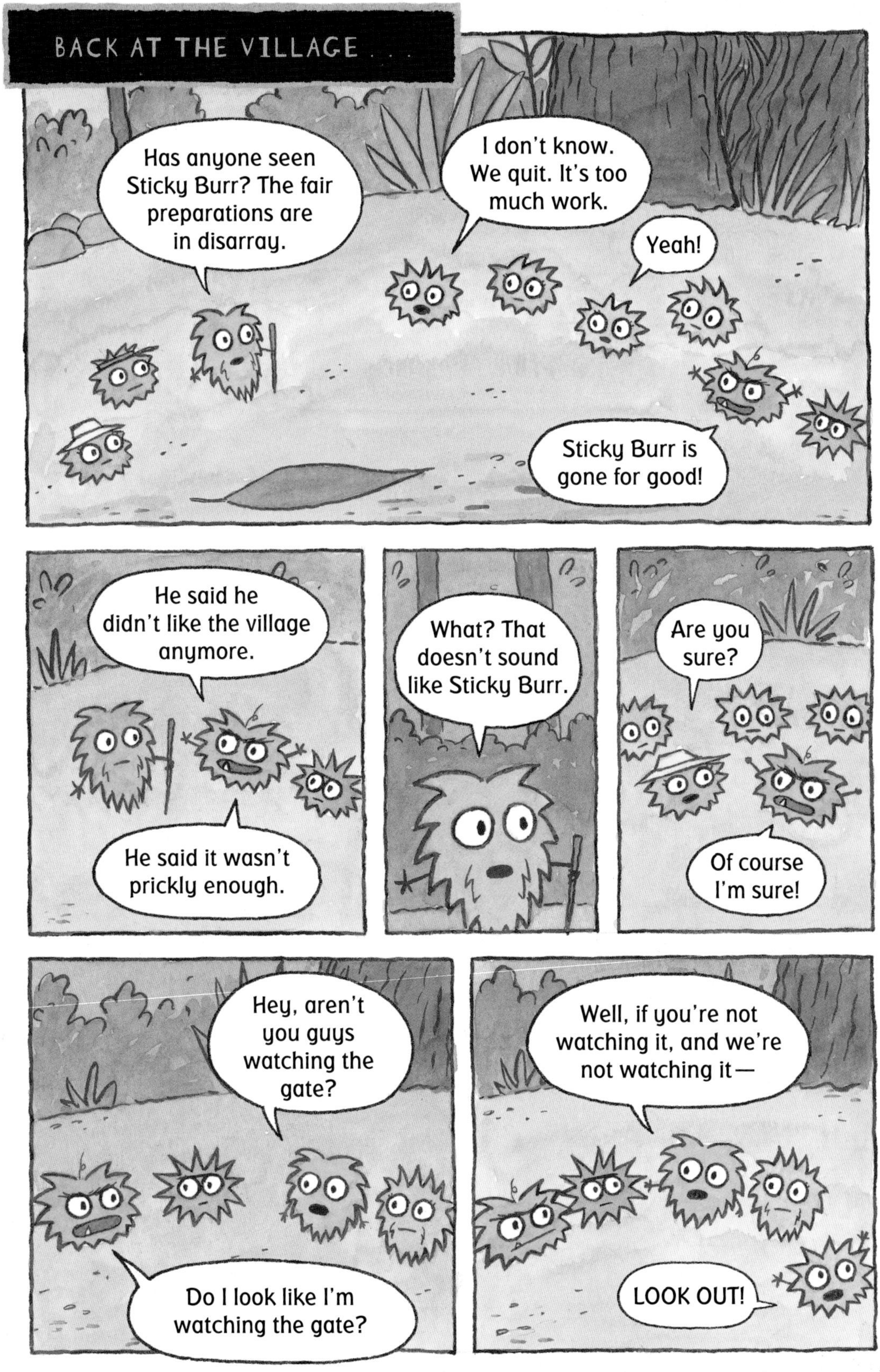
BACK AT THE VILLAGE . . .
Has anyone seen Sticky Burr? The fair preparations are in disarray.
I don't know. We quit. It's too much work.
Yeah!
Sticky Burr is gone for good!
He said he didn't like the village anymore.
He said it wasn't prickly enough.
What? That doesn't sound like Sticky Burr.
Are you sure?
Of course I'm sure!
Hey, aren't you guys watching the gate?
Do I look like I'm watching the gate?
Well, if you're not watching it, and we're not watching it—
LOOK OUT!

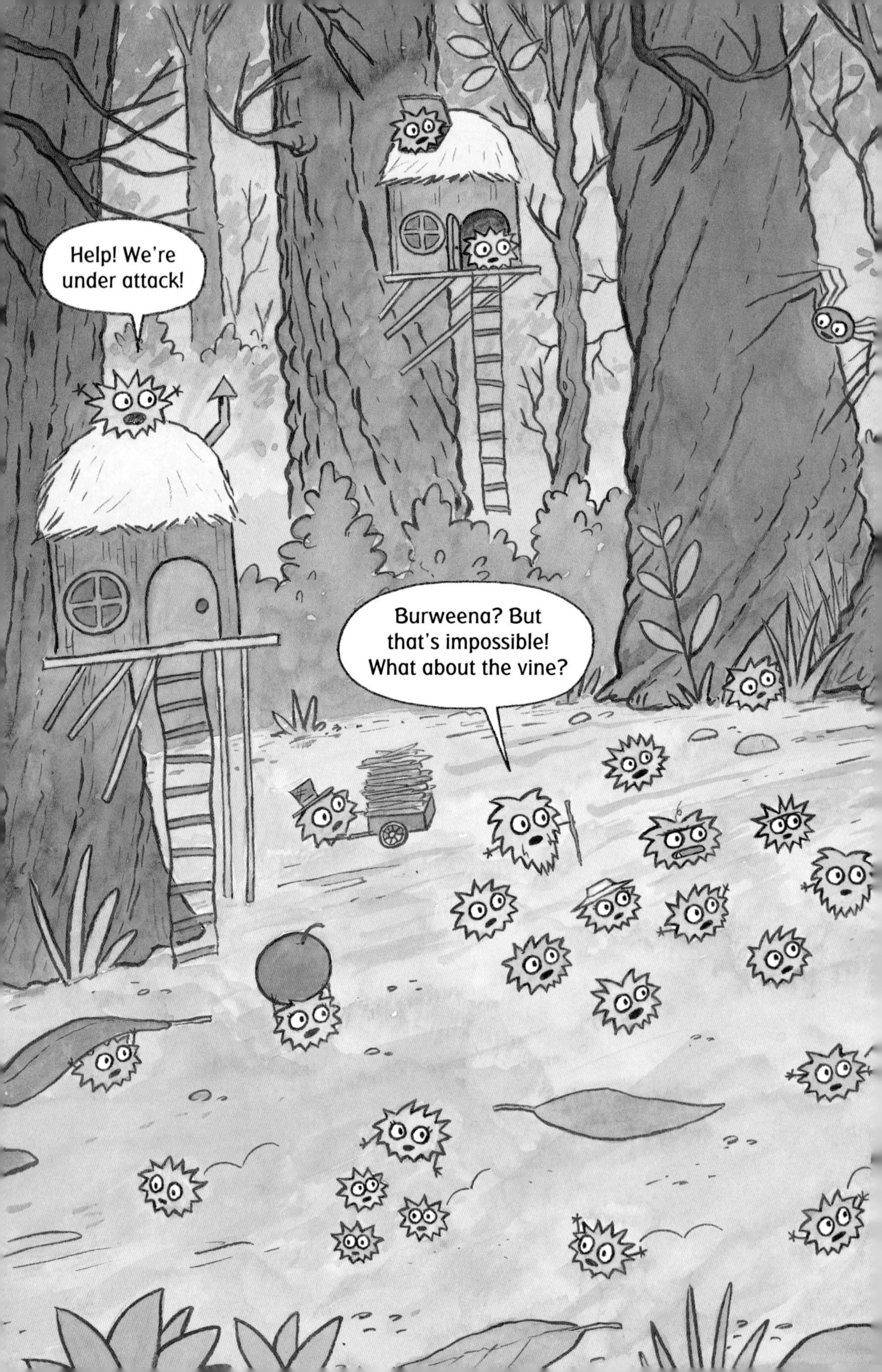
Help! We're under attack!
Burweena? But that's impossible! What about the vine?

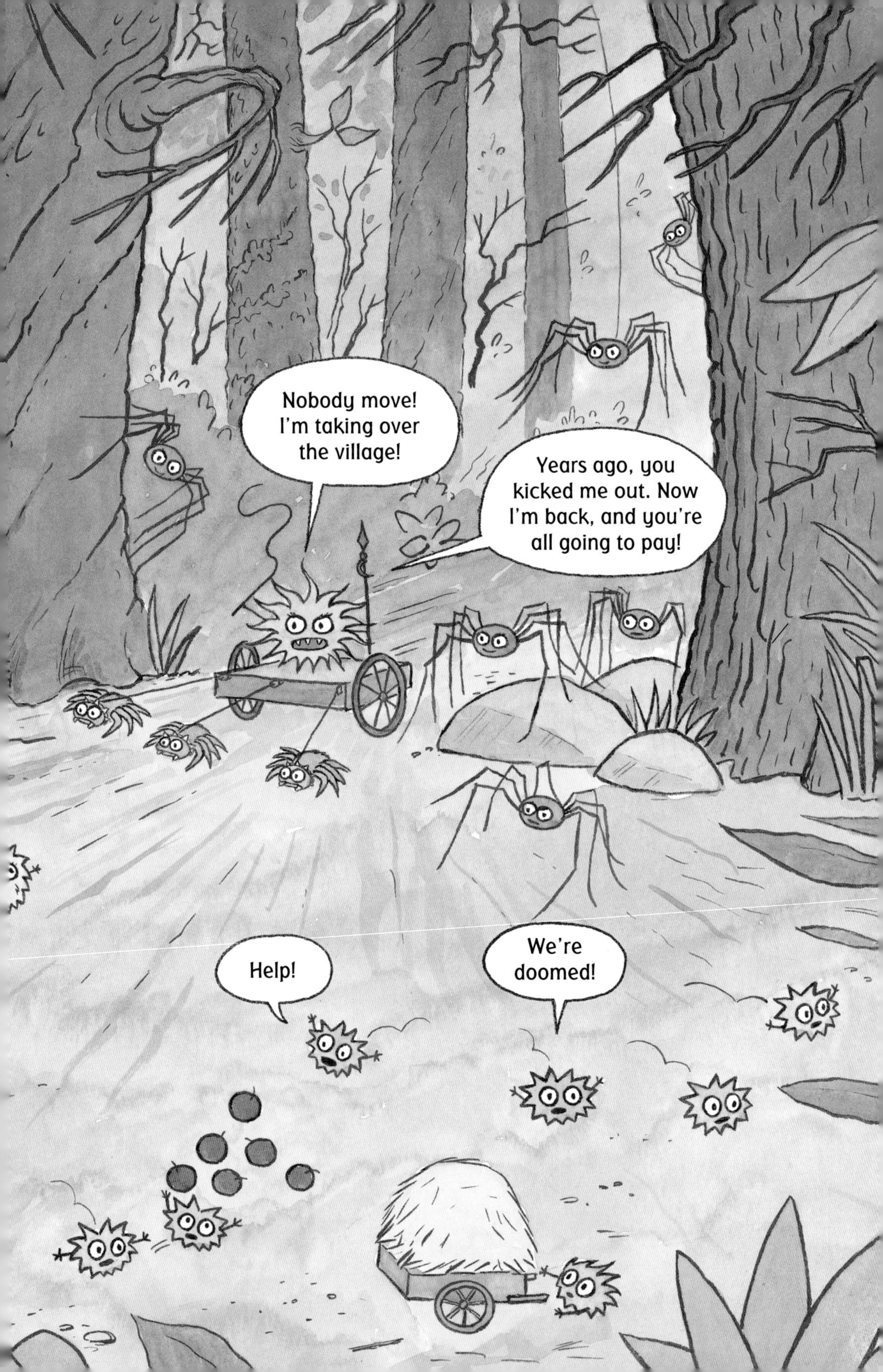
Nobody move! I'm taking over the village!
Years ago, you kicked me out. Now I'm back, and you're all going to pay!
Help!
We're doomed!

A THORNY DEVELOPMENT

I should have
known Burweena
had something
devious planned.
But truthfully, I was
glad that things would finally get more
prickly around here. And I was sure she
would reward me for assisting her.

Me when
I'm happy

AWARD
FOR MOST
PRICKLY

Yes, things were finally looking up.
Unfortunately, though, life can turn
when you least expect it. Like a swirling
breeze on a blustery autumn day . . .

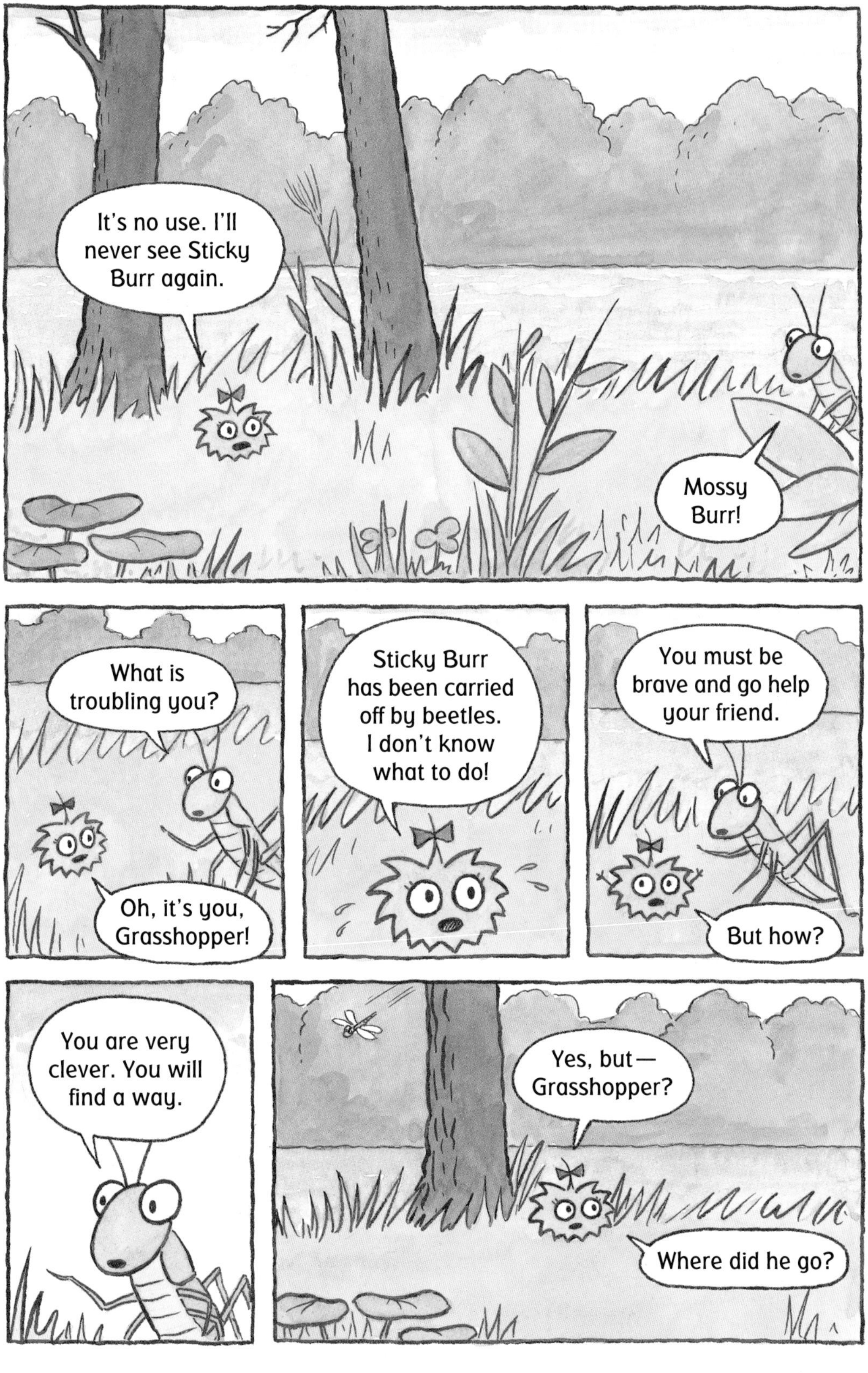
It's no use. I'll never see Sticky Burr again.
Mossy Burr!
What is troubling you?
Oh, it's you, Grasshopper!
Sticky Burr has been carried off by beetles. I don't know what to do!
You must be brave and go help your friend.
But how?
You are very clever. You will find a way.
Yes, but— Grasshopper?
Where did he go?

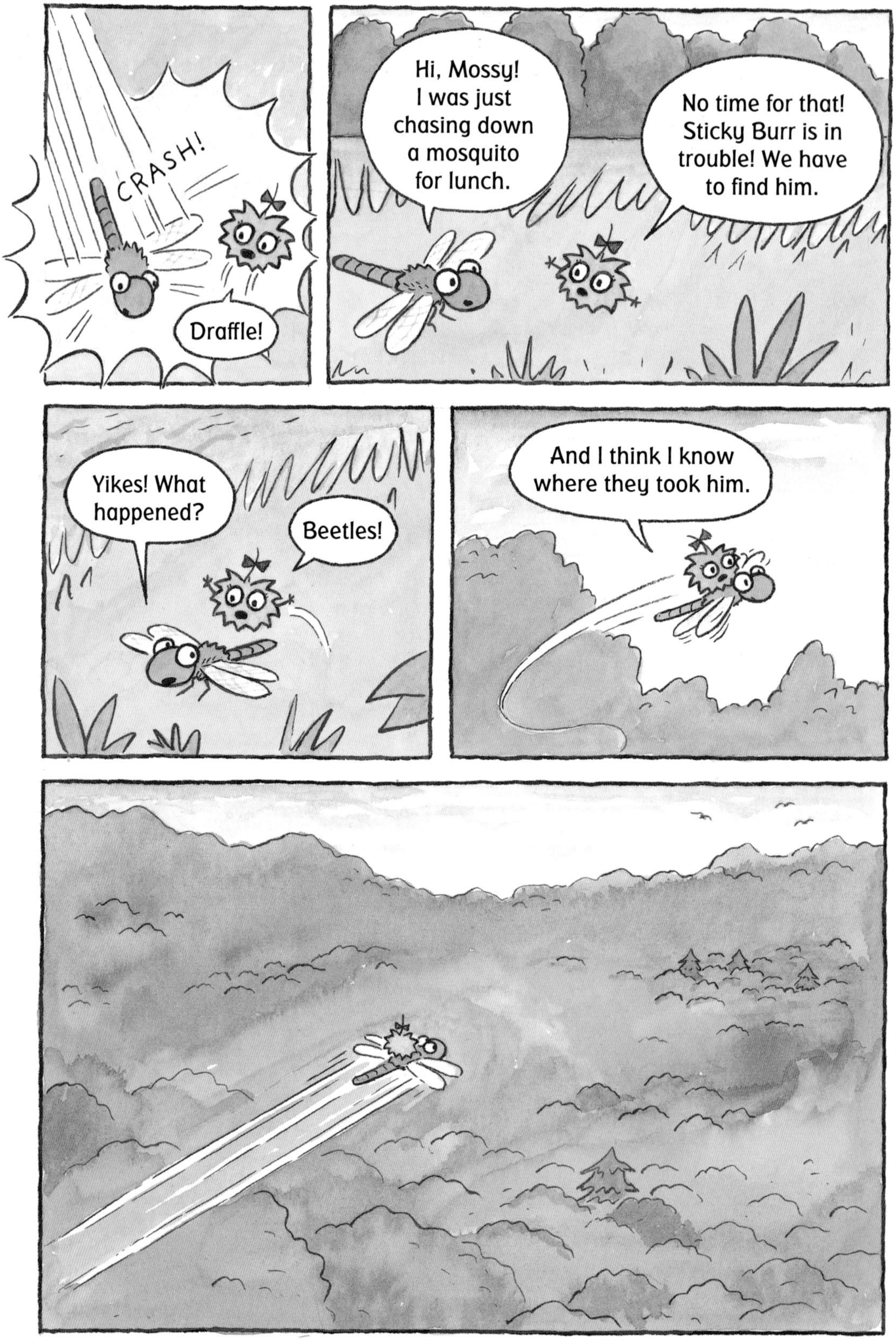
CRASH!
Draffle!
Hi, Mossy! I was just chasing down a mosquito for lunch.
No time for that! Sticky Burr is in trouble! We have to find him.
Yikes! What happened?
Beetles!
And I think I know where they took him.

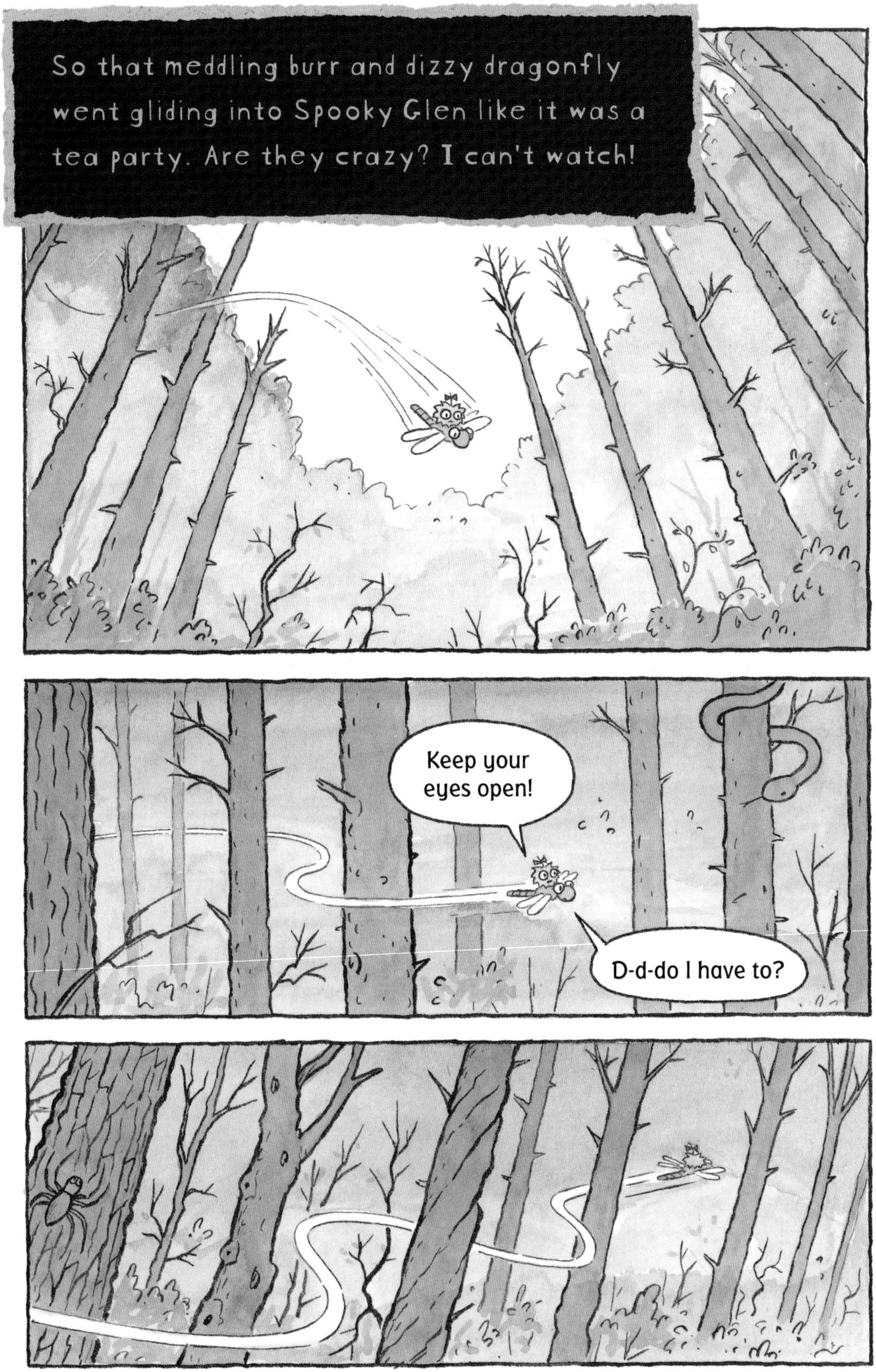
So that meddling burr and dizzy dragonfly went gliding into Spooky Glen like it was a tea party. Are they crazy? I can't watch!
Keep your eyes open!
D-d-do I have to?

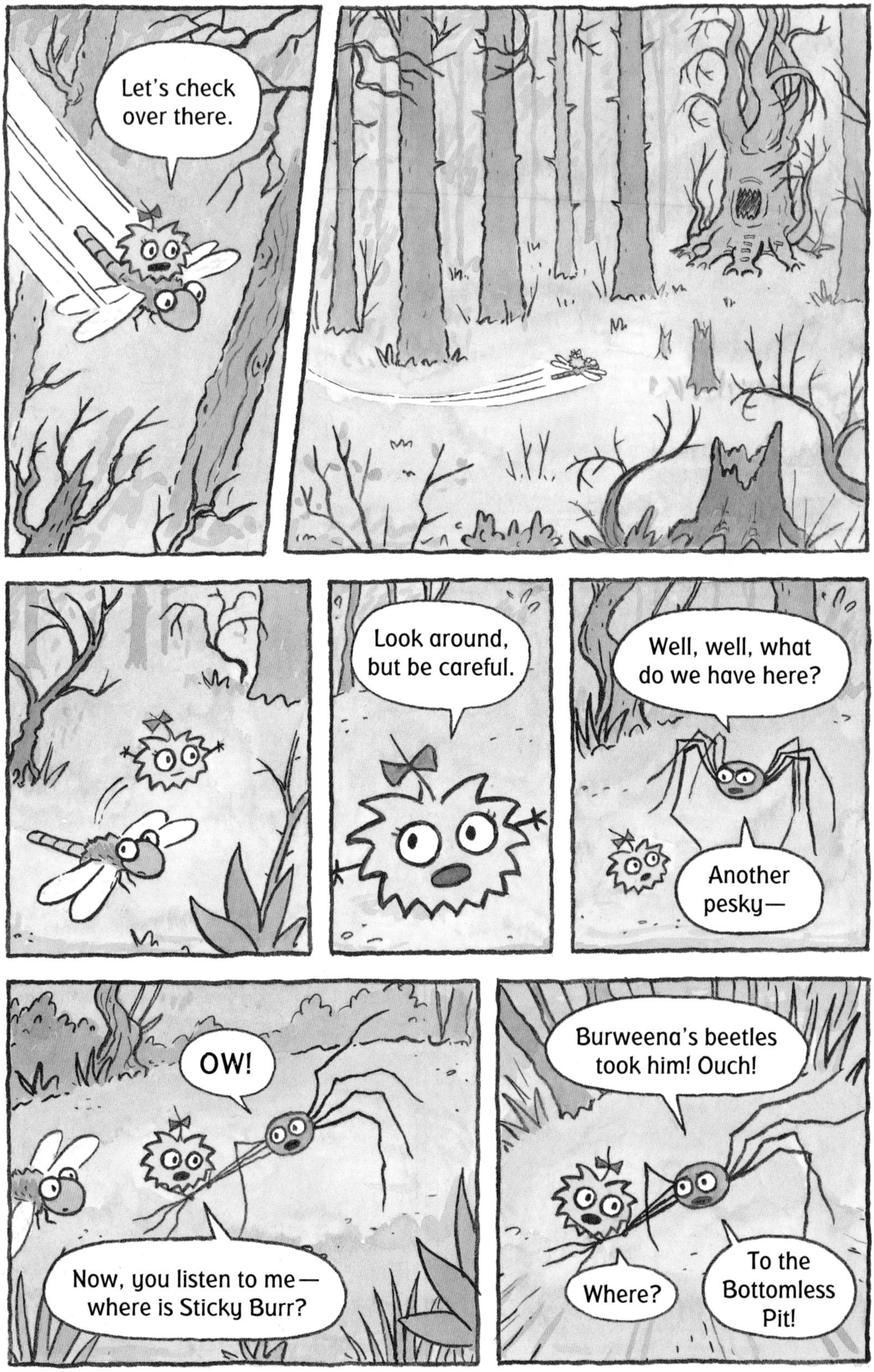
Let's check over there.
Look around, but be careful.
Well, well, what do we have here?
Another pesky—
OW!
Now, you listen to me— where is Sticky Burr?
Burweena's beetles took him! Ouch!
Where?
To the Bottomless Pit!

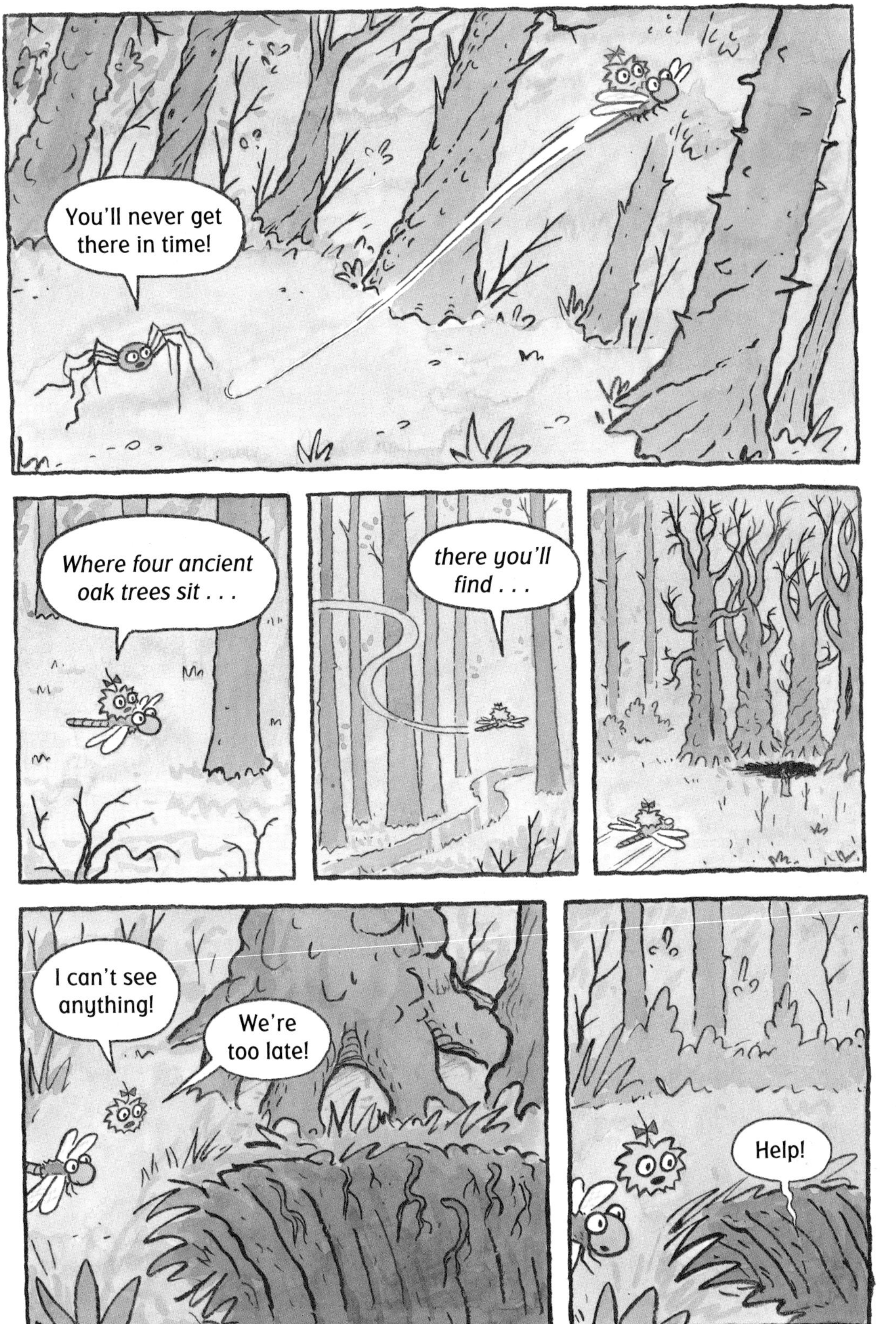
You'll never get there in time!
Where four ancient oak trees sit . . .
there you'll find . . .
I can't see anything!
We're too late!
Help!

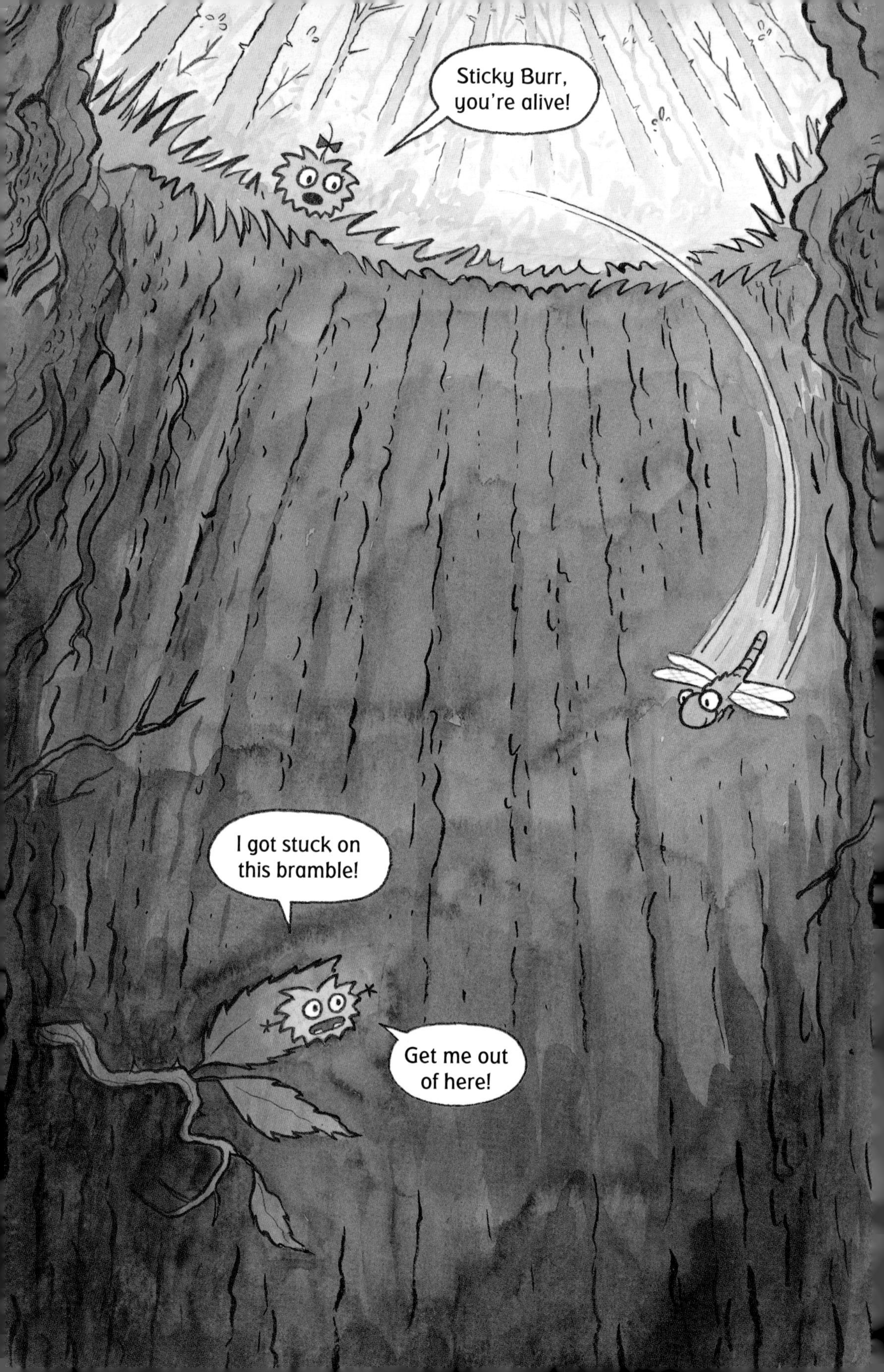
Sticky Burr, you're alive!
I got stuck on this bramble!
Get me out of here!

OH, CRUEL WORLD!

Me in a terrible mood

It's not fair! Somehow Sticky Burr always gets lucky—somehow Mossy Burr always wins. How come I never get lucky? How come I never win?

Whee!

One time, a bunch of us burrs pounced on a muskrat, but he jumped into the river. All the others managed to get off, except me—and I can't swim!

I finally dragged myself to shore, half-drowned, like a mud puppy.

Hi, Scurvy! Taking a swim?

No, you berry brain, I'm picking daisies!

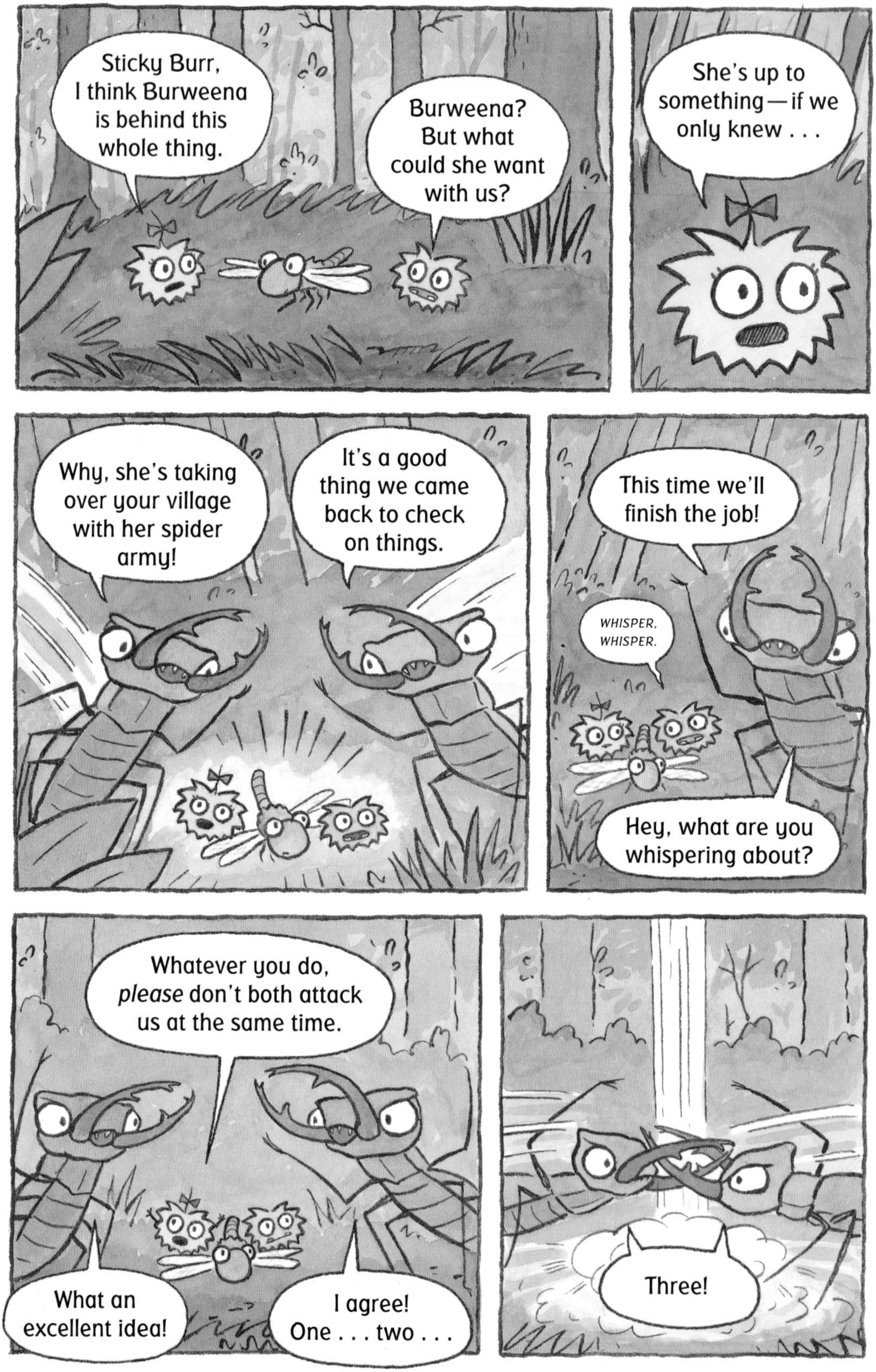
Sticky Burr, I think Burweena is behind this whole thing.
Burweena? But what could she want with us?
She's up to something — if we only knew . . .
Why, she's taking over your village with her spider army!
It's a good thing we came back to check on things.
This time we'll finish the job!
WHISPER, WHISPER.
Hey, what are you whispering about?
Whatever you do, *please* don't both attack us at the same time.
What an excellent idea!
I agree! One . . . two . . .
Three!

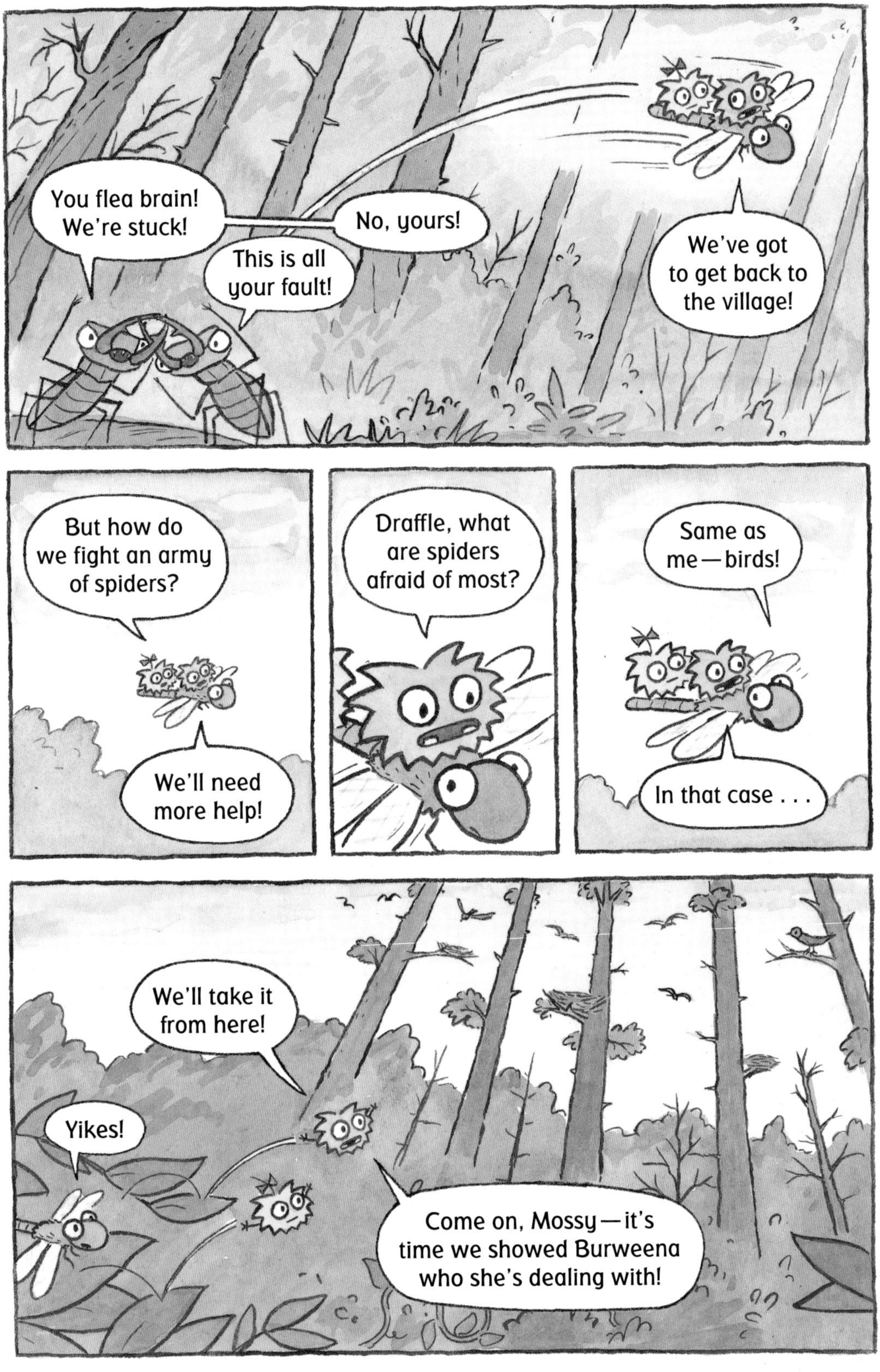
You flea brain! We're stuck!
No, yours!
This is all your fault!
We've got to get back to the village!
But how do we fight an army of spiders?
We'll need more help!
Draffle, what are spiders afraid of most?
Same as me—birds!
In that case . . .
We'll take it from here!
Yikes!
Come on, Mossy—it's time we showed Burweena who she's dealing with!

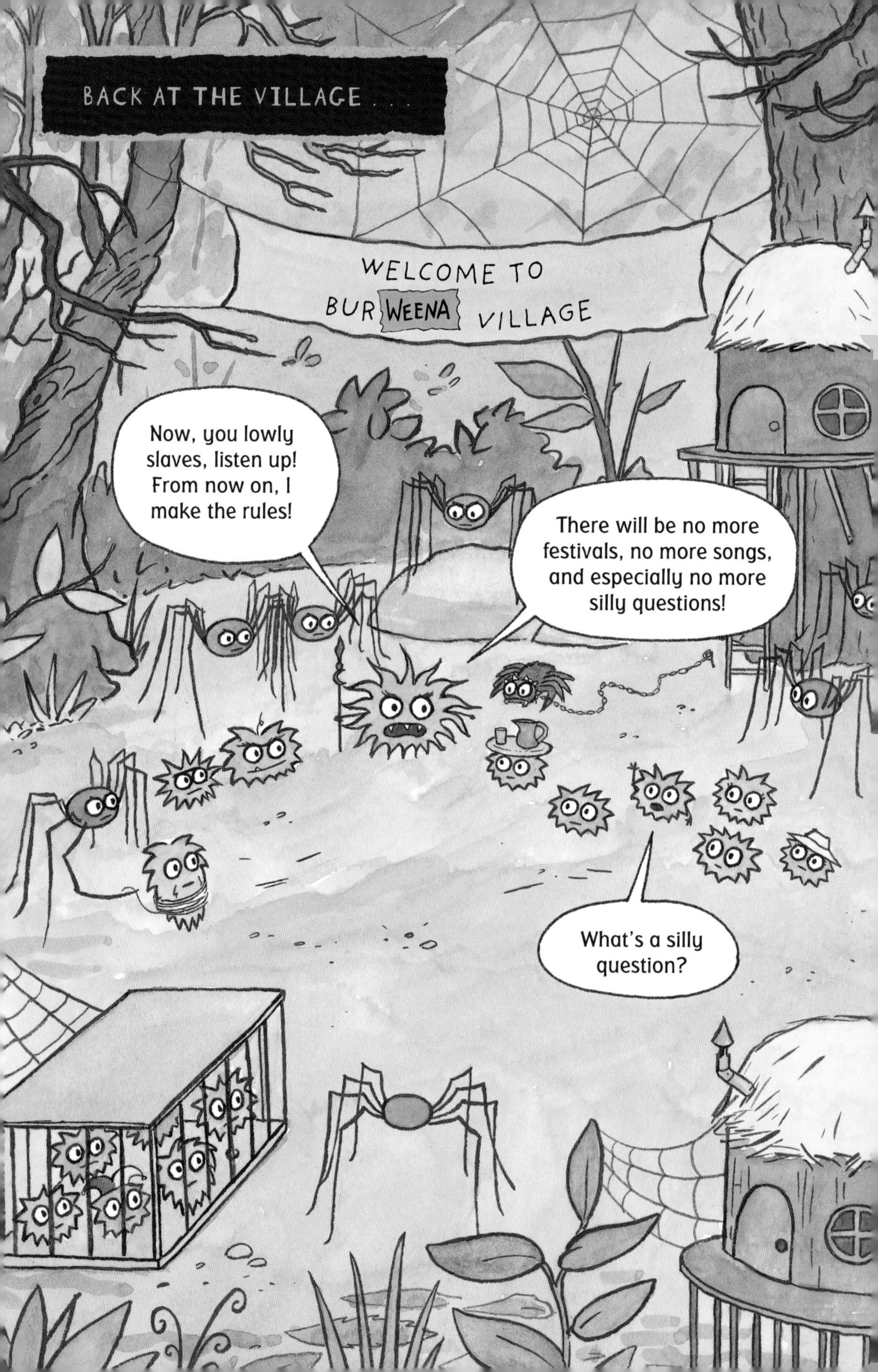
BACK AT THE VILLAGE . . .
WELCOME TO BUR WEENA VILLAGE
Now, you lowly slaves, listen up! From now on, I make the rules!
There will be no more festivals, no more songs, and especially no more silly questions!
What's a silly question?

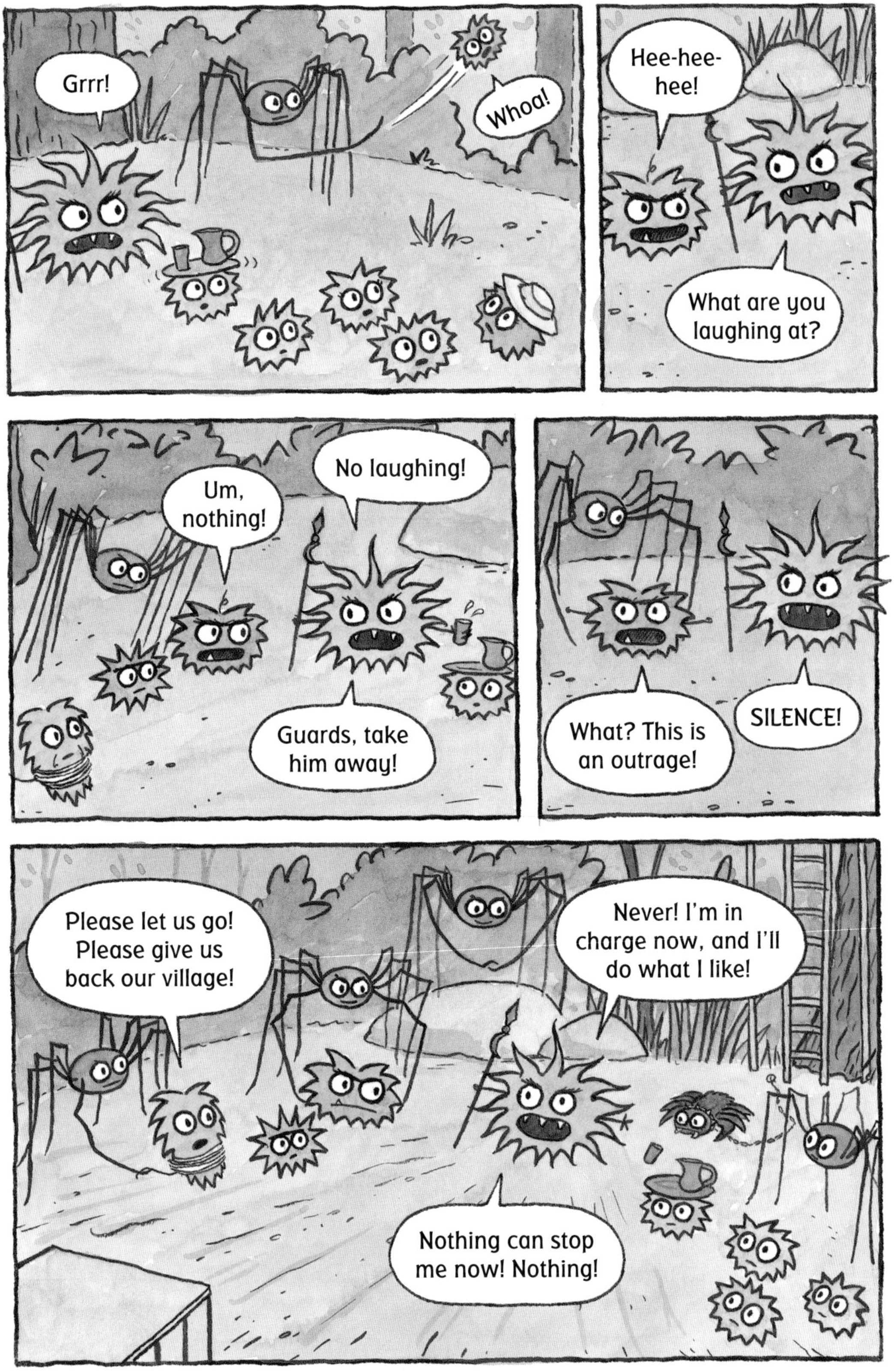
Grrr!
Whoa!
Hee-hee-hee!
What are you laughing at?
Um, nothing!
No laughing!
Guards, take him away!
What? This is an outrage!
SILENCE!
Please let us go! Please give us back our village!
Never! I'm in charge now, and I'll do what I like!
Nothing can stop me now! Nothing!

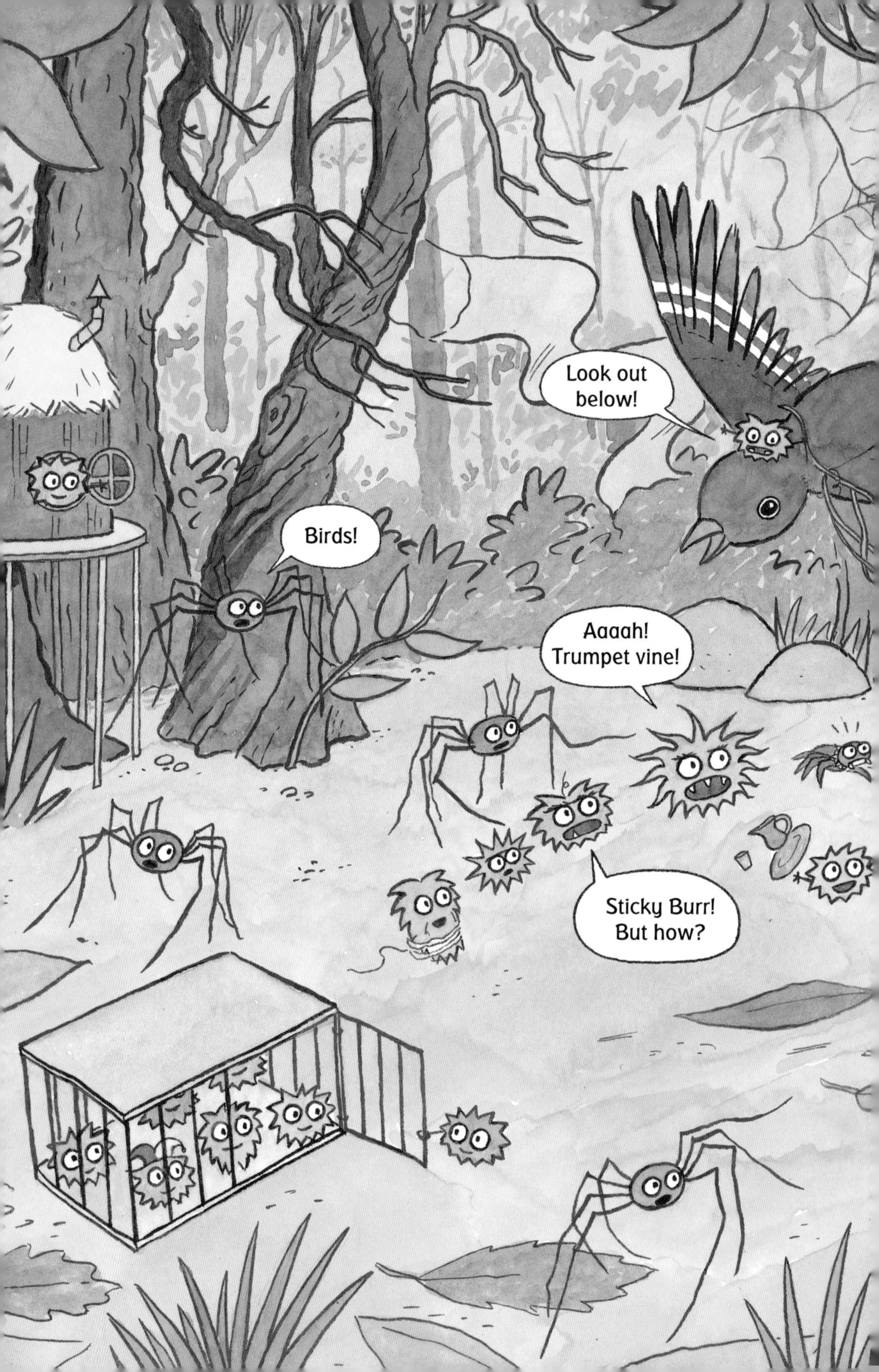
Look out
below!
Birds!
Aaaah!
Trumpet vine!
Sticky Burr!
But how?

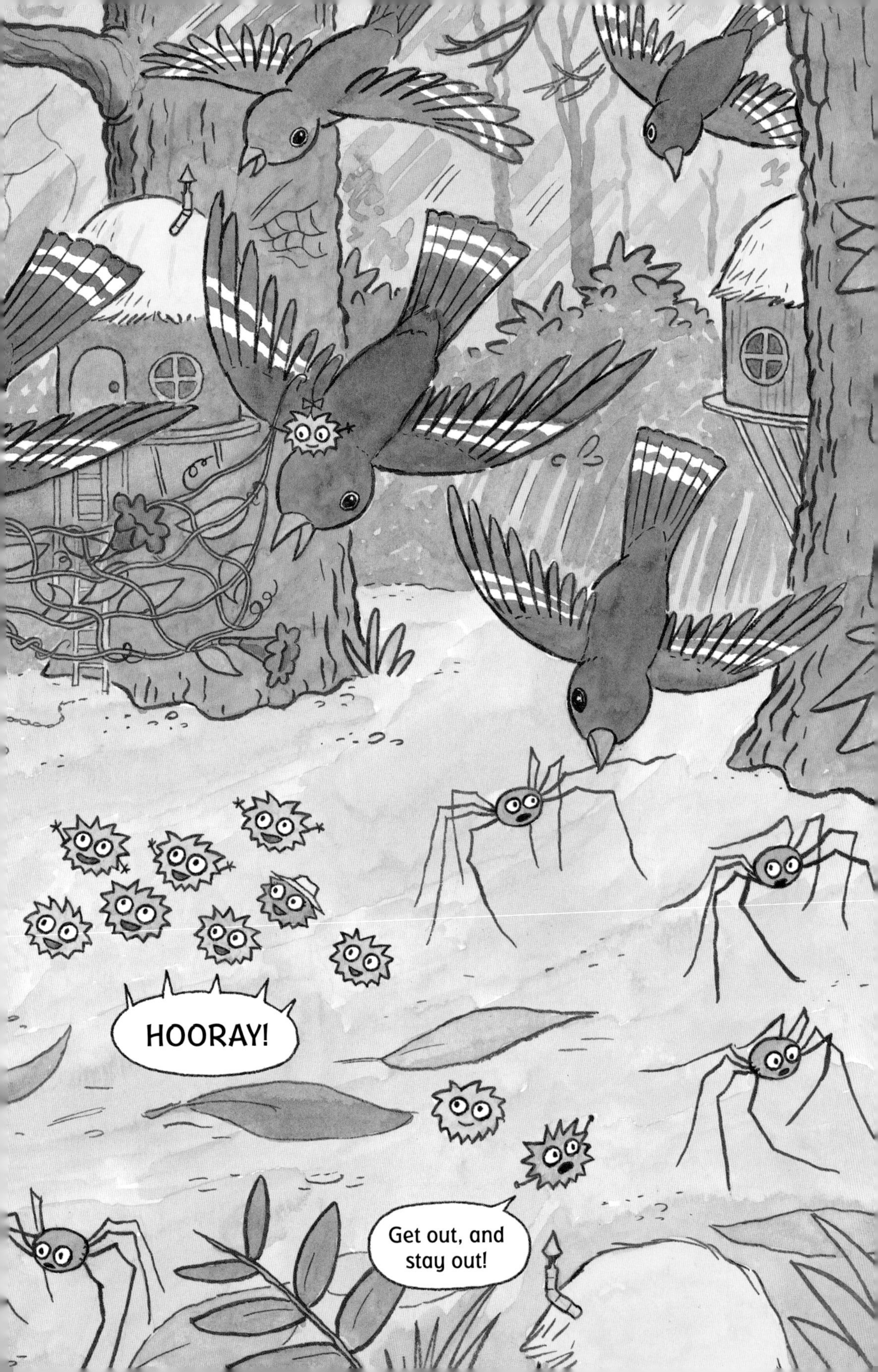
HOORAY!
Get out, and stay out!

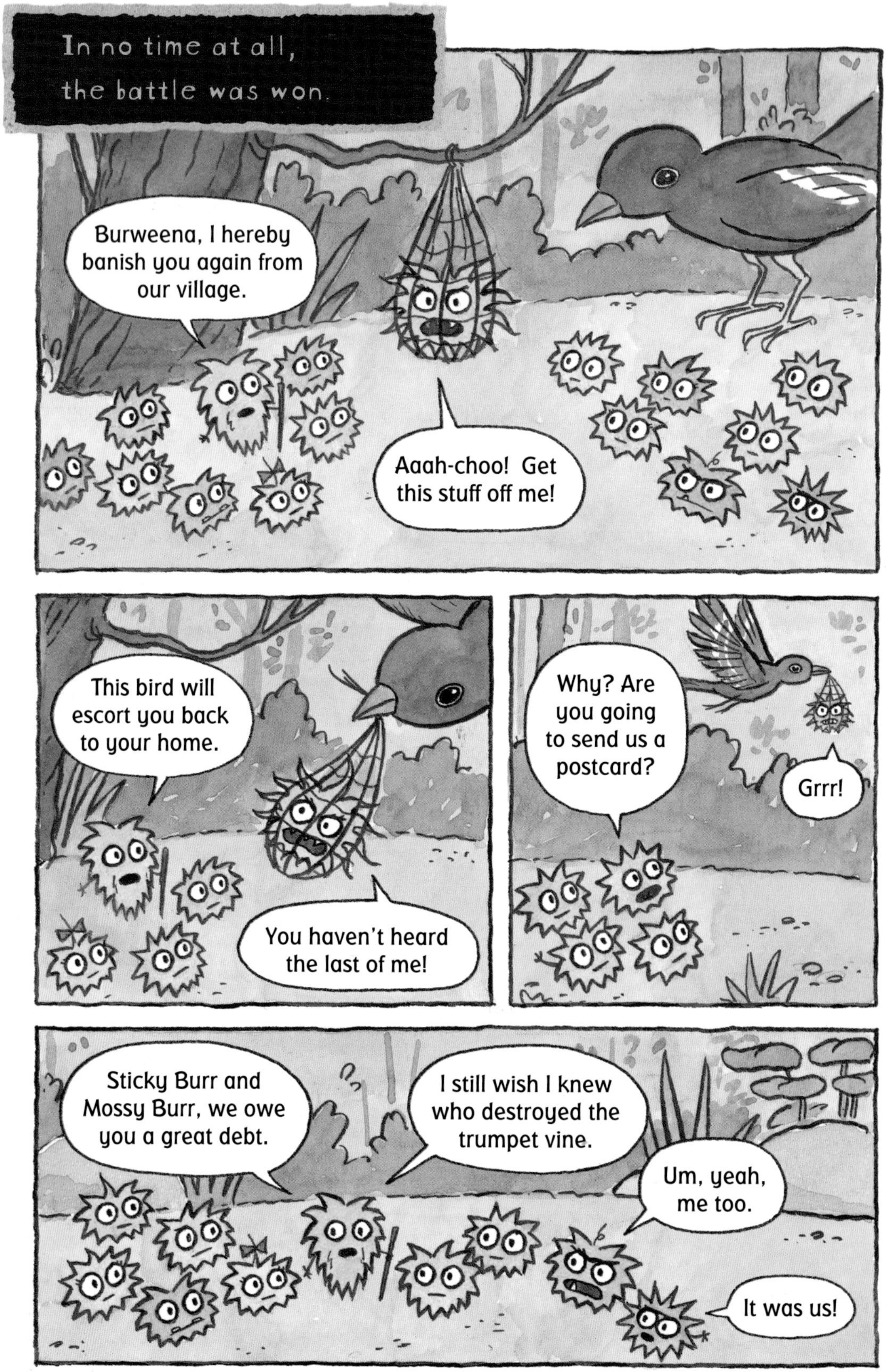
In no time at all, the battle was won.
Burweena, I hereby banish you again from our village.
Aaah-choo! Get this stuff off me!
This bird will escort you back to your home.
You haven't heard the last of me!
Why? Are you going to send us a postcard?
Grrr!
Sticky Burr and Mossy Burr, we owe you a great debt.
I still wish I knew who destroyed the trumpet vine.
Um, yeah, me too.
It was us!

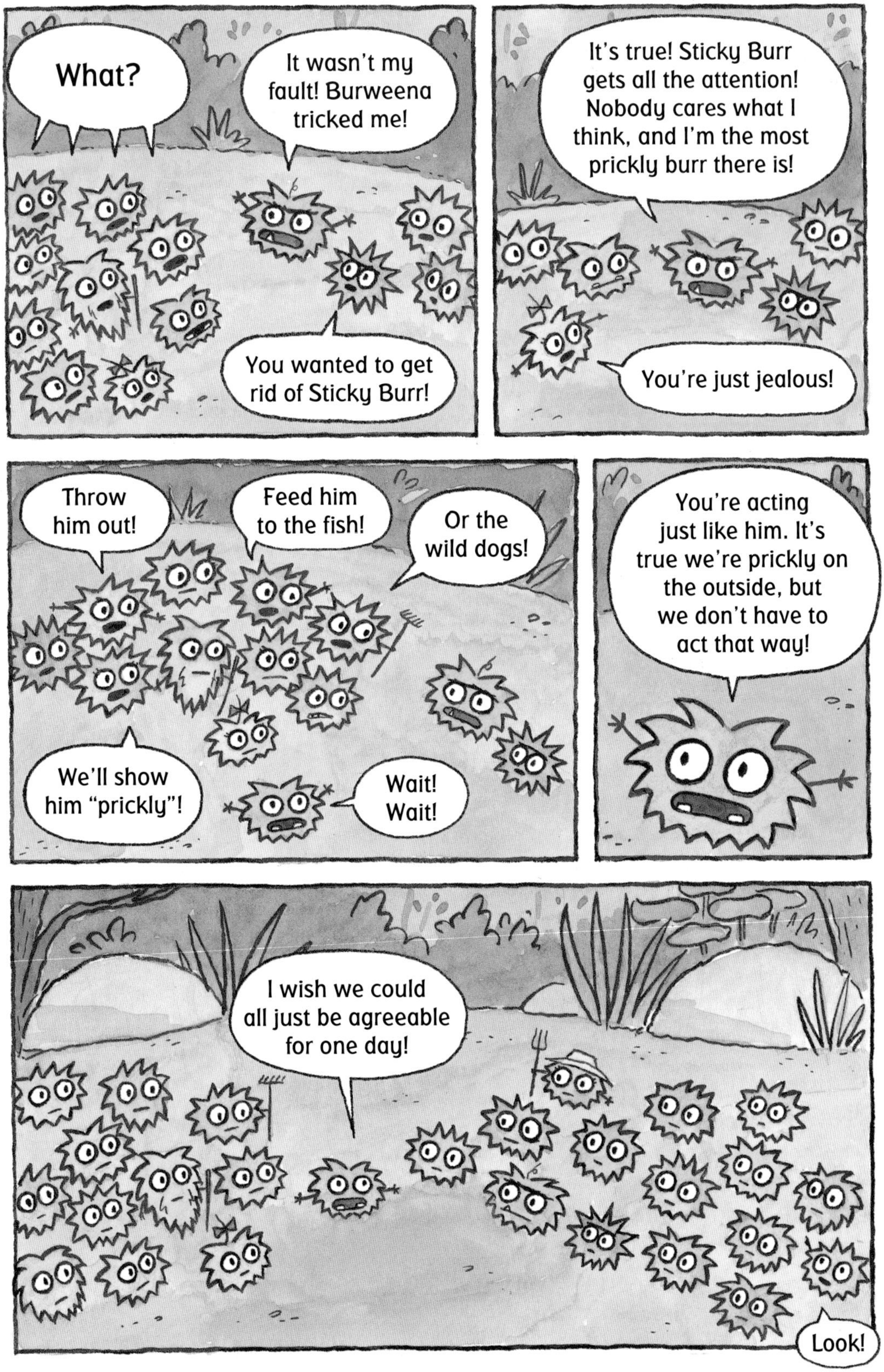
What?
It wasn't my fault! Burweena tricked me!
You wanted to get rid of Sticky Burr!
It's true! Sticky Burr gets all the attention! Nobody cares what I think, and I'm the most prickly burr there is!
You're just jealous!
Throw him out!
Feed him to the fish!
Or the wild dogs!
We'll show him "prickly"!
Wait! Wait!
You're acting just like him. It's true we're prickly on the outside, but we don't have to act that way!
I wish we could all just be agreeable for one day!
Look!

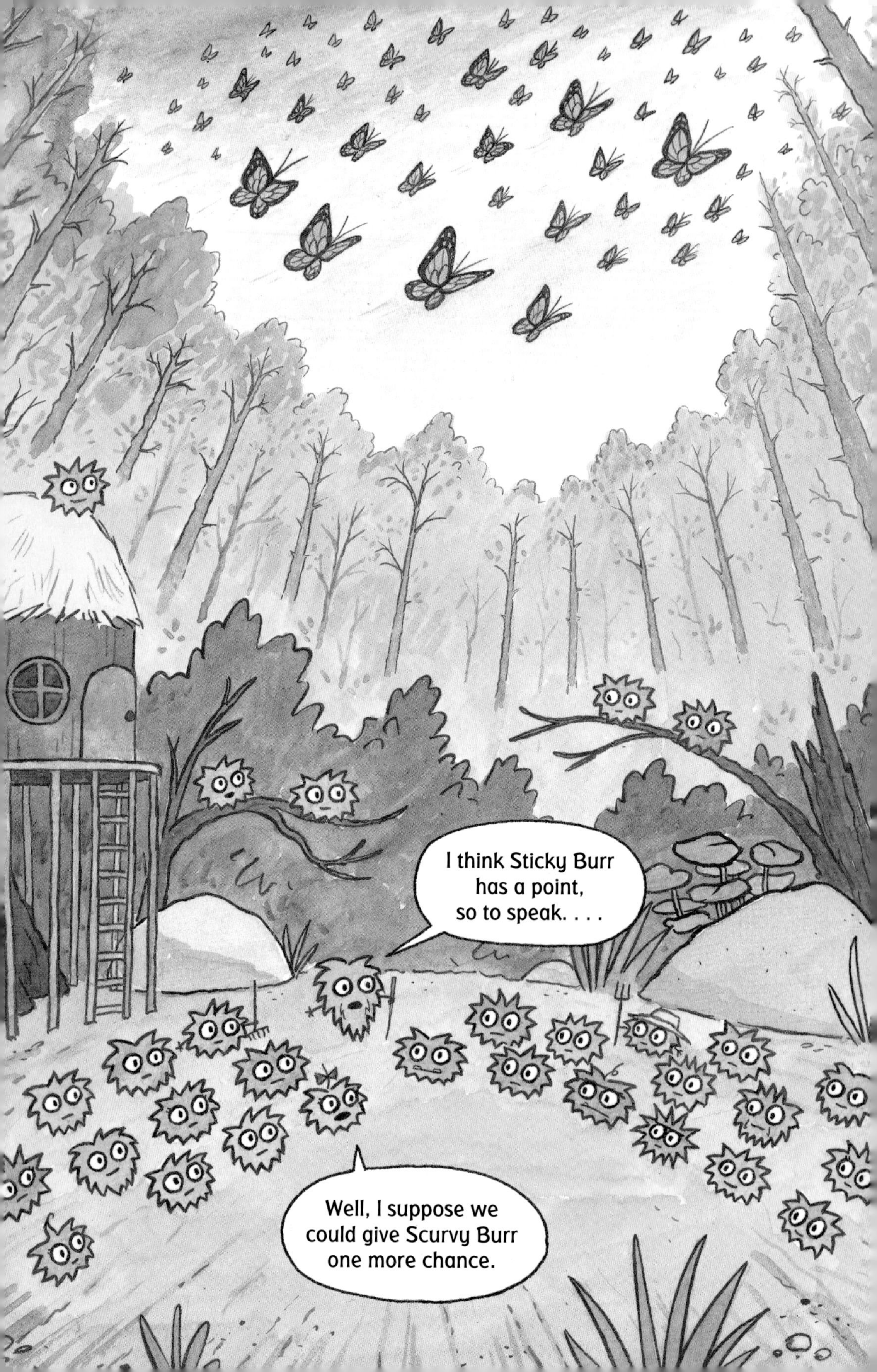
I think Sticky Burr has a point, so to speak. . . .
Well, I suppose we could give Scurvy Burr one more chance.

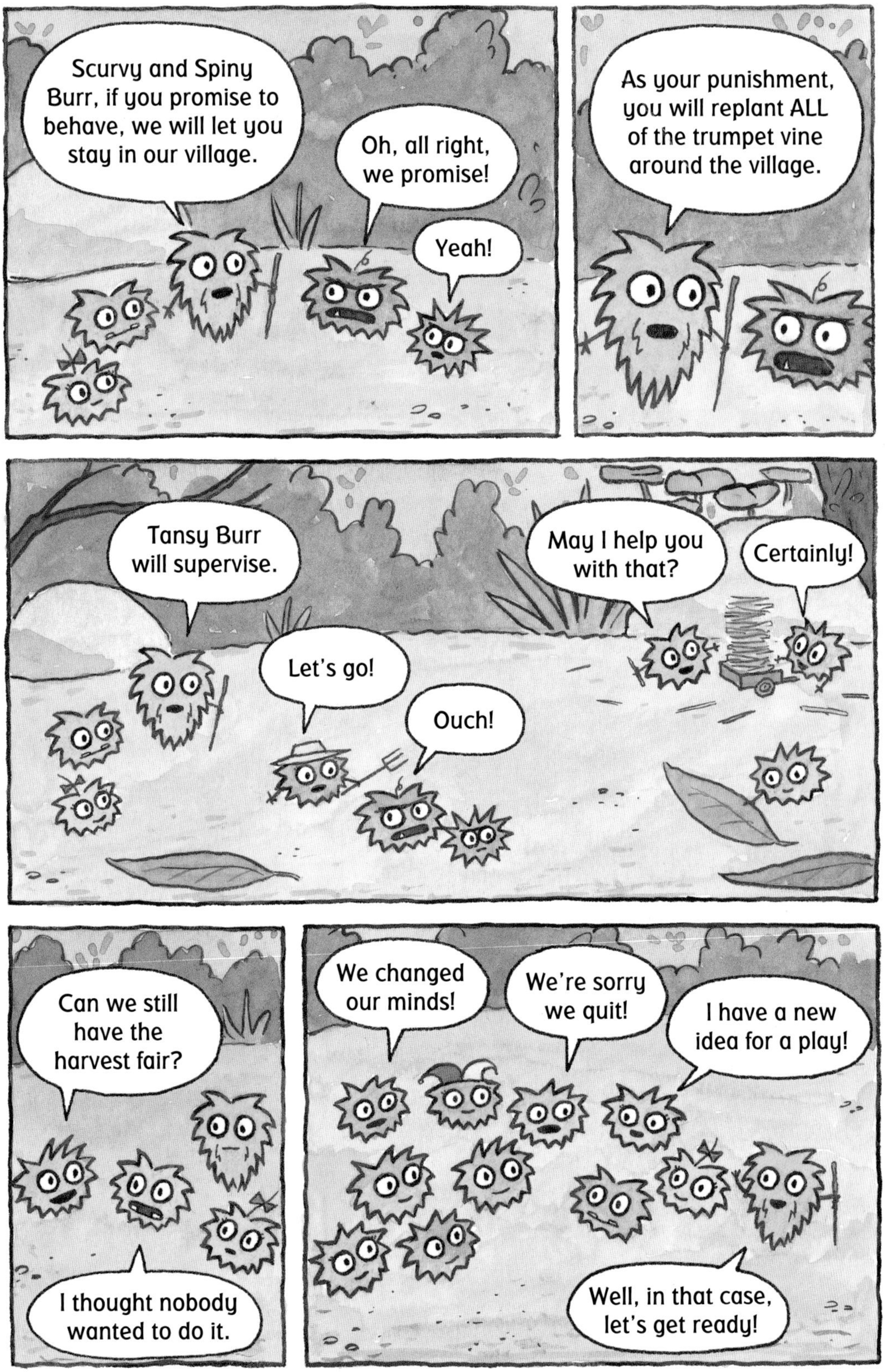

Scurvy and Spiny Burr, if you promise to behave, we will let you stay in our village.
Oh, all right, we promise!
Yeah!
As your punishment, you will replant ALL of the trumpet vine around the village.
Tansy Burr will supervise.
Let's go!
Ouch!
May I help you with that?
Certainly!
Can we still have the harvest fair?
I thought nobody wanted to do it.
We changed our minds!
We're sorry we quit!
I have a new idea for a play!
Well, in that case, let's get ready!

So the burrs had their silly harvest fair. After I finished planting the vine, they even let me judge the prickly pear contest, so I guess it wasn't all that bad.

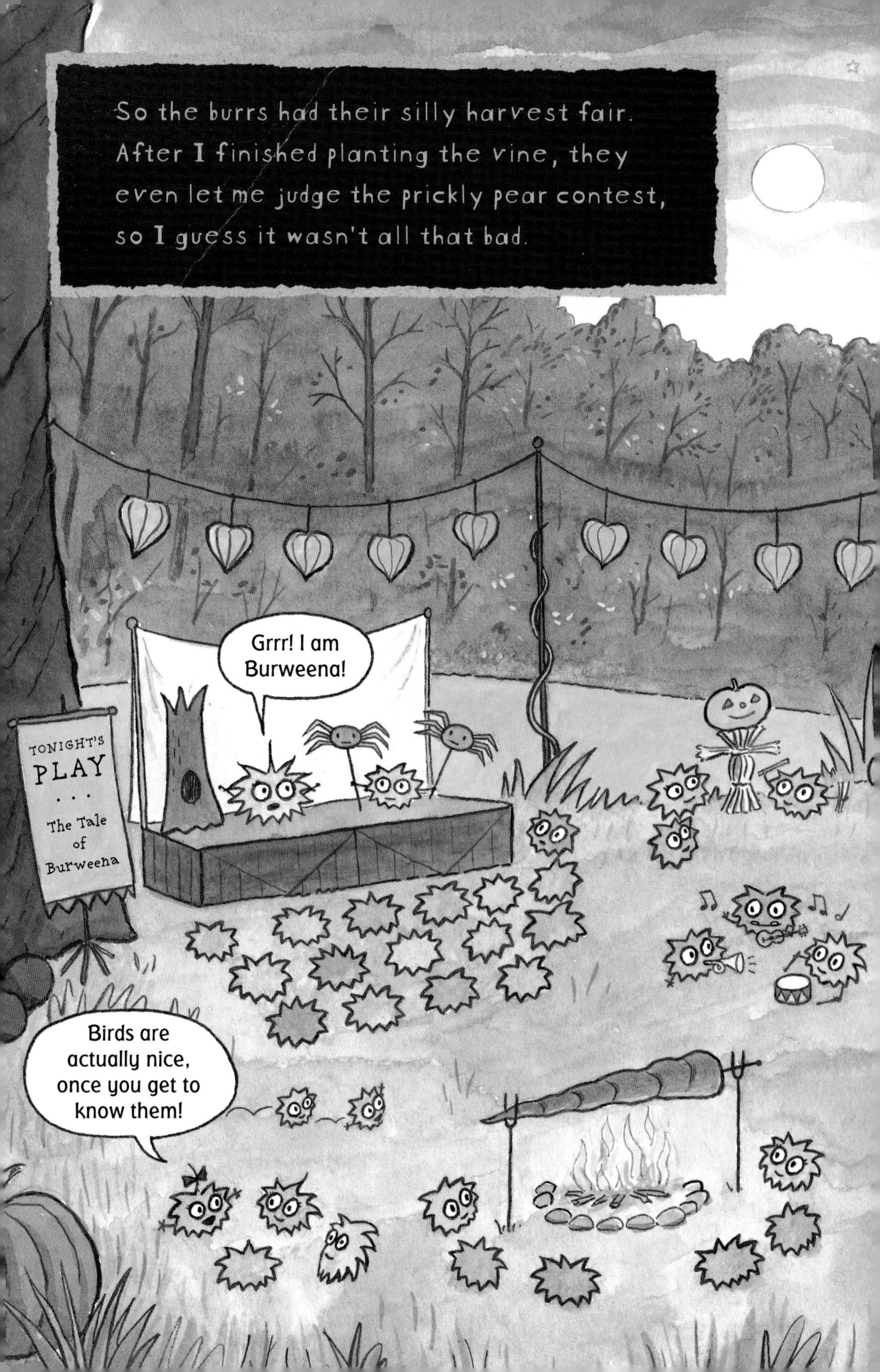
Grrr! I am Burweena!
TONIGHT'S PLAY . . . The Tale of Burweena
Birds are actually nice, once you get to know them!

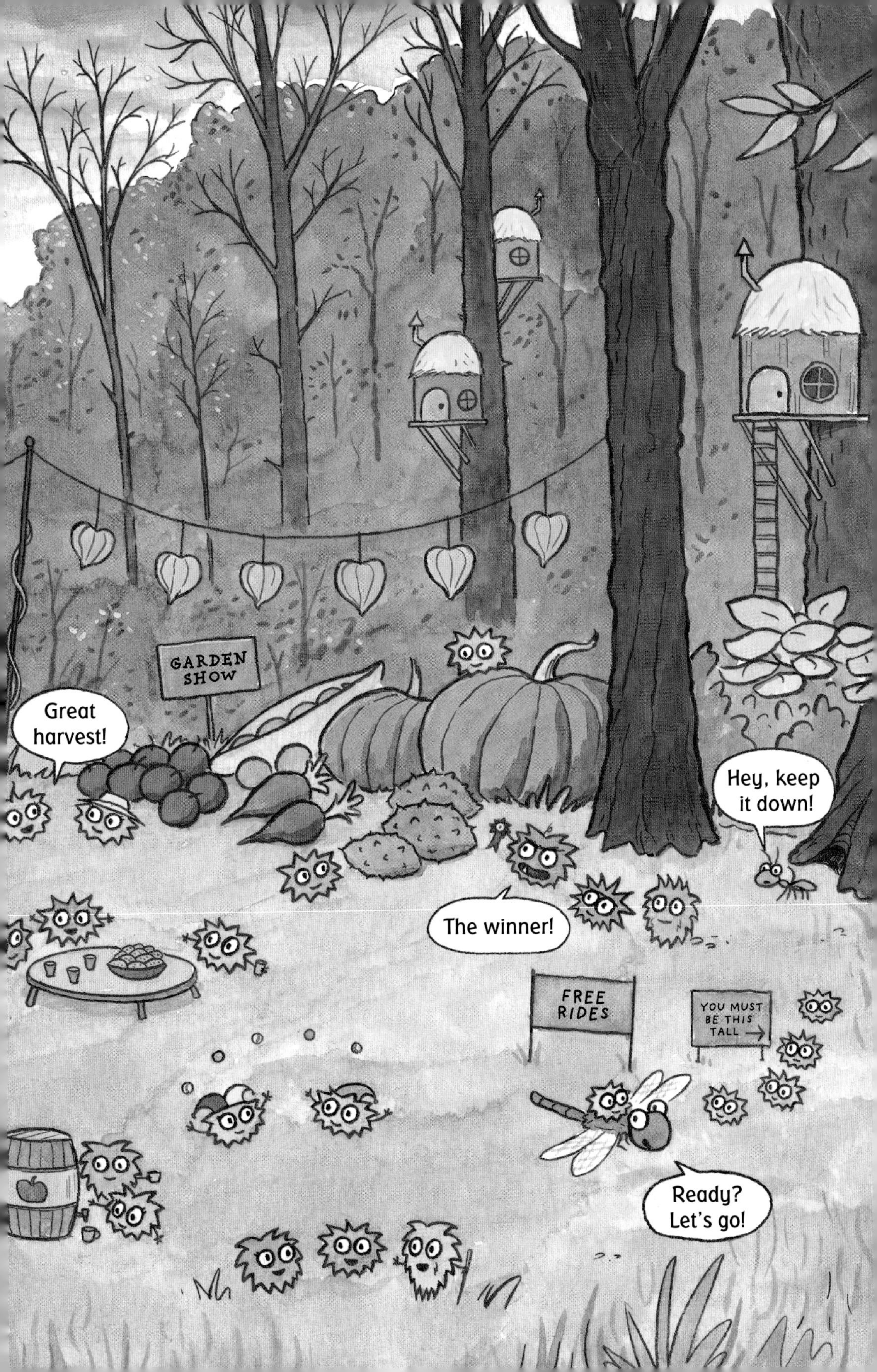
GARDEN SHOW
Great harvest!
Hey, keep it down!
The winner!
FREE RIDES
YOU MUST BE THIS TALL →
Ready? Let's go!

THE FINAL SAY

Well, Sticky Burr got his wish, and all the burrs were nice for one day.

But how long can it last? If a seed is prickly when it falls off the tree, isn't that how it's meant to be? It can't just change into something different—or can it?

Grrr, these questions are making my brain hurt. I'm going to curl up in my cottage, light my stove, and wait for winter to come. So there!

EPILOGUE

Wow . . . that was—
Colorful!
Original!
And surprisingly accurate!
It was better than YOU could do!
Look, guys!
I have a new pet! His name is Jumpy!
Aww . . . cute!
That does it. I'm leaving!
THE END
Whoa!

Scurvy Burr's PRICKLY GUIDE

In case you ever come to Burrwood Forest, I'm going to show you the most prickly places to visit!

Yeah!

1. Spooky Glen: This is the most wild and beastly place in the forest, full of sharp things. The beetles and spiders won't bother you if you don't bother them.

Beetle

Spider

Porcupine

2. Pine Ridge: If you like prickly pines and jagged rocks, this is the place for you! I come here to eat pinecones.

3. Home of the Wild Dogs: This place is dry and rocky and full of sharp thistles. Watch out for the dogs. They are downright mean!

Dogs like bones!